Just

Under

Nine

Just Under Nine
©2016 by Matthew McCain

This is a work of fiction. All characters and places are the products of the author's imagination. Any resemblances to actual people or locations are purely coincidental.

Edited by: Judy Morgan Murphy
Proof read by: Barbara Muller

Cover image: Shutterstock/Prazis

Published by Piscataqua Press
142 Fleet St.
Portsmouth, NH 03801

www.ppressbooks.com

ISBN: 978-1-944393-28-1

Printed in the United States of America

Just Under Nine

A Novel

Matthew McCain

To Nate and Matt Wootten:
For teaching me at a young age that it's okay

And for Sue:
An angel like no other R.I.P.

I: Tears

The sky had completely clouded over as twenty-four-year-old Garrett Allan drove up his mother's long dirt driveway in Auburn, New Hampshire. The weather had held out long enough for the funeral but it was clear just from the sky that it was going to rain at some point. But it wasn't the weather that was on Garrett's mind; that was the last thing he cared about. The only thing on his mind was the last time he saw his best friend. No matter how hard he tried, he just couldn't stop thinking about that last night he had spent with Matt.

When he got to the end of the driveway he put the Chevy pickup in park, but instead of getting out and heading inside to his mother Pam and girlfriend Katie he stayed in the new truck, trying to somehow shake off the feeling of shock that was all around him. But he just couldn't. No matter how hard he tried, the wounds of his heart felt just as fresh as they did when he first found out about Matt.

At first when he saw the posts on Facebook, he thought it was a prank—some sick joke that someone thought would be funny—but it wasn't. And when he was told that it was indeed true, Garrett lost it, breaking his record of not crying after seven years. But Matt dying wasn't the worst part about the whole situation; the worst part was how he died. It was that piece that haunted him the most, the part that he simply couldn't accept.

For a brief moment while he was sitting there, Garrett started to remember back to that last night they were together, trying to pick up on any warning signs he might've overlooked...but nothing came to mind off the top of his head. In fact, as searched through his memories of those final moments, he thought Matt had seemed in good spirits. He was so lost in thought, he didn't even notice Katie walk out of the house and over to the truck.

Just by the look on Garrett's face, Katie could tell that Garrett was in pain. It surprised her because, for the past two and a half years they've been together, she's had a difficult time trying to not only read but also understand how Garrett deals with his emotions. From the surface it looks like Garrett has absolutely no emotions at all. But his face in the truck proved otherwise.

"Hey," she said gently.

Garrett—feeling like he was showing his softer side—quickly cleared his throat and began getting out of the truck, despite feeling sick to his stomach.

"Hey." He closed the truck door and looked at Katie as he began loosening up the black tie that was around his neck before she leaned in and put her arms around his waist.

Garrett returned the gesture as he exhaled deeply, trying not to really attach himself to what had been going on the past few days, but it seemed to be an impossible task.

"You okay?" Katie asked as she held Garrett in her arms.

"I'm okay," Garrett said in a much softer voice than how he normally spoke.

Katie knew for a fact that he was only saying that so she wouldn't worry about him, but she also knew that it wasn't the time or place to call him out for lying. She decided to let him be and give the illusion that she believed him on this one.

"Okay...as long as you know I'm here if you need anything," she said before kissing him on the cheek.

"I do. Thank you," he said back with a light smile across his boyish-looking face.

Katie suddenly took her eyes off Garrett and looked up when she felt a few small raindrops land on her blonde hair.

"Why don't we go in? You're Mom and I made you a little something," Katie said, trying to sound chipper.

Garrett forced a smile and walked toward the country house they were staying at while they saved up for a place of their own. They both tolerated living with Pam—Garrett's mom—for the most part. Everyone seemed to put their issues and past behind them while they saved for an apartment somewhere around the area. Between a car, motorcycle, and phone payment it was tough for them to really save a whole hell of a lot, but they were slowly reaching their goal, close to about halfway when Garrett got the news.

Garrett's relationship with his Mom was still a sore subject at best; everyone in the house knew that. Garrett (for the most part) was always one for giving everyone a chance. Even with such a shitty childhood he learned to do that...but Pam used up her chance a while back...along with the dozens of other ones Garrett's given her along the way.

Between Garrett finishing up high school and Pam raising a newborn, for a while they didn't even talk to each other, aside from the once in a while phone call or text message...they both drifted apart with time. A choice that neither of them wanted and yet neither one chose to fix. But for some unknown reason, they both decided to simply reconnect a few months back. Neither one of them said it out loud, but they were happy to be back in each other's lives, despite both knowing it probably wouldn't last much longer.

Garrett's childhood was rough to say the least. Pam had him while she was still a kid herself: sixteen. Garrett's father, Dan, was also a kid when Garrett was born, and he couldn't find it within himself to rise up and help raise Garrett the way he should have. He left even before Garrett was born...a choice that affected Garrett strongly once he was old enough to realize that his own father walked away.

Pam did her best to raise Garrett but it was hard. It sounds awful, but some people aren't ready to put their life on hold for a child, although that's what a child requires the most: time. Some people just don't have the time to give, and at that point Pam didn't have the time (or even patience) to give...so she didn't.

It was Garrett's grandparents who watched and pretty much raised him in his baby years, while Pam worked and then went out to live life. It seemed to work out well for both of them, until both his grandparents were killed in a car accident. The accident broke Pam's heart, but it was Garrett who lost the most in that moment. The two people that watched over him and made sure he was always safe were suddenly gone. But that wasn't the only change Garrett had to deal with then, either.

Not long after the death of her parents, Pam found out that she was pregnant once again, only this time with twins. The news was just another weight thrown on top of Garrett's young shoulders. There's no denying it was tough for him, being so young and yet having to act so much older. By the time the twins were born, Garrett's brief childhood was nothing more than a distant memory.

As the twins grew up and Garrett got older, Pam increasingly took time off from her home life and went out doing what she wanted, leaving Garrett behind to care for the twins. While Pam went out partying and drinking after work,

Garrett made sure the twins, Autumn and Junior, got home from school safely, did their homework, made them dinner, bathed them, and put them to bed...by himself...every night...for years on end. Pam kept a roof over their heads, but it was Garrett who made it a home.

But as he reached high school, it was clear Garrett was getting tired of having to be a parent to his brother and sister. Unfortunately, instead of listening to what her son had to say, Pam called Garrett selfish, and shouted that he should be thankful. Just before she kicked him out of the house, Garrett left on his own, moving in with his Uncle Pete.

On that day a lot of things were said, things mothers should never say to their sons and things sons should never call their mothers. That day and those words ended their relationship for almost two and a half years. And in that time a lot of things changed, for each of them, only they just didn't know it...yet.

II

Garrett walked into the warm yet messy countryside house. He instantly smelled one of his favorite dishes: shepherd's pie.

Ever since he was a young boy living off of Cartier Street on the east side of Manchester, shepherd's pie had been his favorite dish. Every time he smelt it in the air, memories would race through his mind from when Pam, on the rare occasion she was home, would make it for him and the twins.

"Smell good?" Katie asked as she helped Garrett out of his black jacket.

Garrett nodded as he looked into the living room where Pam's boyfriend, Jeff, was watching T.V. Jeff could tell just by Garrett's face how he was feeling, so Jeff decided to only nod his head at him instead of their normal handshake. Garrett returned the gesture.

"Pam, he's back," Katie said as they walked into the kitchen.

Garrett cleared his throat and followed her as the smell of his favorite meal grew stronger and stronger. The lighting in the kitchen was far from good. The gloomy white sky didn't help bring in any light from the windows either, but it was still enough light for Garrett to have a difficult time hiding how he was feeling.

"Hey kiddo," Pam said as she looked up from the oven, checking on the chocolate chip cookies.

Garrett forced a smile on his face just before Pam walked over to him and gave him a hug.

"How you holding up?"

"Fine," Garrett said, lying through his teeth.

Pam shook her head, choosing to ignore the lie. "I am sorry...I know he was your best friend. If you need anything I'm here; we're both here for you," Pam said as she looked at Katie.

Garrett nodded.

"I know...thanks, Mom."

Pam patted Garrett on the shoulder and gave him a quick wink.

"You hungry?" She asked. "Made you your favorite. And Katie made you your favorite snack."

"Chocolate chip cookies! Made with love...and swears, because I couldn't get the goddamn beater to work," Katie said.

Garrett chuckled.

"The twins are on their way over and we're all going to have dinner together, so if you're in the mood to eat you're welcome to join us," Pam said.

"No, don't really have an appetite. I was actually planning to go see Uncle Pete now," Garrett quickly said.

Pam nodded with a slight smile despite not being entirely thrilled about him going to see Uncle Pete.

"Okay then, you think you'll be back tonight?" Pam asked.

"Yeah, I'll be back," Garrett said as he walked out of the kitchen and into his room.

As he entered the messy room, he began taking off his white cotton dress shirt and his black pants. Katie walked quietly into the bedroom and softly closed the door.

"I'm worried about you," she said.

"Don't be," Garrett said as he tossed his pants on the floor.

"Your best friend just died. Of course I'm going to worry about you. I'm worried that you're going to start blaming yourself," Katie confessed.

Garrett sighed with aggravation.

"Like I said, don't be. I'll deal with it in my own way. Like I do with everything else," he said firmly as he put on his brown shorts.

Katie eyes began to water.

"I know, that's what I'm afraid of. You can't deal with this by keeping everything bottled up like you do. I know he was a good friend and was an awesome guy, but..."

"You say that like you knew him. You've never even met him. You have no idea the kind of person he was...and if you don't know that, then you have no idea how difficult it is to grasp the fact that the funniest guy I've ever known killed himself. I know you're trying to help, but please...just leave it alone," Garrett said.

Katie shook her head as tears ran down her cheek.

"I'm sorry...I was just trying to help."

Garrett put on his grey and red running shoes and then looked at Katie. He exhaled deeply when he saw how upset she was. He walked over to her and then gave her a hug.

"Hey, I'm sorry. I don't mean to sound like an asshole...I just don't know where to go from here. I need time to think," Garrett said before kissing her on the top of her head.

"Do you want me to go with you to Pete's?" She asked.

"No...it's best if I go by myself. He's probably in bad shape himself. He knew Matt just as well as I did."

Katie nodded her head.

"Okay. Just know that I love you."

"I know. I'll be back later on," Garrett said as he grabbed the keys to his truck and walked out of the bedroom.

"You leaving?" Pam asked as Garrett walked past her.

"Yeah, I'll text you when I'm on my way back home."

"Okay. Drive safe."

"Bye," Garrett said as he walked out of the kitchen and toward the front door.

As he left the house and got into his truck, Pam and Katie watched him, both trying desperately to somehow figure out his state of mind.

"I'm worried about him," Katie broke the silence.

"He'll be okay...just give him time," Pam said.

But even though Pam was trying to remain positive, deep down she knew that Matt's death was a devastating blow for her son. Not only because they we're best friends, but also because of something she thought a while back about Matt...and if it was true, Garrett was more of a wreck than anyone could imagine.

III

While Garrett got into his truck and headed into Manchester, Garrett's Uncle Pete walked into his apartment on Cartier Street. Like Garrett, he also was dressed up for the funeral, but quickly began taking off his collared shirt the moment he reached his top floor apartment. His girlfriend of eight months, Erin, wiped tears from her eyes when she heard Pete come in.

Erin had only known Matt for just over five months, but in that short time she quickly fell in love with his sense of humor and big heart. The news of Matt's death was mind-blowing for her, but Pete had known Matt for almost seven years. She knew he was in far worse shape than she was in. Like Garrett, Pete usually kept everything inside, burying it as far down as it could go. But unlike Garrett, Pete learned early on in life that no matter how hard you try, some things just can't be buried. Matt's death was one of those things for Pete.

As he opened the refrigerator to grab a beer, the thought of Matt dying by his own hands started playing in his head. His entire body froze with shock as his mind painted the haunting picture in his head. The thought was so strong and crippling, the bottle of beer slipped through his hands and smashed on the floor, glass crashing everywhere as tears began to fill his eyes.

"What happened?" Erin asked as she ran into the kitchen, fearing the worst.

"Nothing, just dropped my beer," Pete said as he reached back in the fridge and grabbed another one.

Erin walked over to Pete and gave him a hug.

"Go on and relax, I'll clean this up," she said as she patted Pete on the back.

Pete nodded his head and forced out a smile, something that he hadn't done in weeks.

"Thanks..." Pete softly said as he cracked open his beer and then walked toward the living room.

As he walked away, Erin couldn't help but watch him. Just by the way he was moving, it was obvious that he was heartbroken—lost like so many others that had known Matt. Erin was heartbroken too, but she did her best to force her emotions to the side so she could be strong for Pete. She told herself she would deal with her own sadness later on. But her train of thought was interrupted by Pete's cell phone suddenly ringing.

"Hello?" Pete asked in a deep voice.

"Pete, it's Pam."

"Hi Pam. Sorry I've been meaning to call but I just got in...how's Garrett doing?"

"He says he's okay but I know he's lying."

"Yeah...yeah he probably is. But you know how he is..."

"Yeah I do...anyway I wanted to let you know that he's on his way to see you...left about twenty minutes ago."

Pete sighed. "Okay, thanks for the heads up."

"I need a favor from you Pete," Pam bluntly said.

"Okay..."

"He talks to you...he looks up to you. Please be there for him. If he talks to anyone, it's going to be you."

"I will. You have my word."

"Thank you Pete," she said as she began to sniffle.

"Well, I just got home, so I'm going to change before he comes over, I suppose."

"Okay, I'll let you go then...but Pete?"

"Yeah Pam?"

"Thank you for filling in for your brother. Don't think I've ever said this to you before but Garrett is lucky to have you."

"No problem. I'll talk to you later."

"Okay...bye."

As soon as Pete hung up the phone he let out a big sigh, knowing what was about to happen.

"Was that Garrett?" Erin asked as she walked back in.

"No, that was Pam letting me know he's on his way over here."

"She say how he was doing?"

"Yeah, he keeps saying he's fine. So I know what that means...he's probably going to crack here."

Erin nodded her head.

"We all do eventually," she said, remembering how she had held Pete when he found out about Matt.

Pete nodded, then walked over to Erin and put his arms around her before kissing her forehead.

"Thank you for being here for me. I know this isn't easy for you either," he said.

"I'll always be here for you. And don't worry about me."

"You're starting to sound like Garrett," Pete said with a soft chuckle.

"You know what I mean," she said and softly punched Pete in the stomach.

"Well I better get ready for when he gets here, so we can get this over with."

"Okay, babe."

"You know I've always taken care of him, tried to make sure I'm strong for him. But this is different, not sure how I'm going be strong for him this time, when I feel the exact same way," Pete confessed.

"Just take it one step at a time. That's all you can do," Erin said; wishing she could provide a better answer.

"We'll see, I guess," Pete said before walking into the bedroom.

As he started to undress and put on his normal clothes, he couldn't help but feel bad, not only for Matt but also for Garrett. Matt may have lost his life, but Garrett lost his best friend, his companion and possibly more. Pam had an idea, but it was Pete who had more than just a feeling. He was almost sure...and that's why he was so concerned for Garrett.

II: Questions

Autumn and Junior pulled into the driveway at Pam's house. Like most siblings, the two of them always seemed to be in an argument, mostly because Junior didn't like the way Autumn drove. But the car ride that day was a lot quieter than usual. Both of them had also known Matt: Junior not as much, but Autumn on the other hand, had really gotten to know him.

"I thought Garrett was supposed to be here?" Junior said.

"Maybe he's on his way," Autumn said.

"Did he text you back?"

"No, he didn't pick up when I called, either. Kinda expected that though." She shut off her car and then checked her phone again.

Junior shook his head as he opened the car door and got out. "What do you think we should do?"

"Just give him space. He's going to be distant for a while,

anyway. Can't say as I blame him either," Autumn said, trying to make sure her brother had as much private time as she could provide him with.

"Yeah, still feels weird. I know I haven't seen Matt in a while, but he was fun to be around...funny too."

Autumn smiled as a thought or two of Matt popped into her head.

"Yeah he was," she said, thinking about when Matt was over for dinner and the food Pam cooked was worse than awful, so he carefully fed most of his plate to their dog Moose while Pam wasn't looking.

"How are you?" Junior asked, pulling Autumn out of her memory.

"Huh? How am I with what?"

"With Matt...you know. You saw him more than I did, so this can't be easy for you either..." Junior said as they walked toward the house.

"Haven't really thought about it, honestly. Just doesn't feel real yet. I mean, I know it will and when that happens I'll be a wreck, but right now...I don't know. I guess I'm still waiting for his orange car to pull into the driveway like it always does," she admitted.

Junior shook his head and looked up. The cloudy sky was very slowly starting to break up, exposing patches of light blue.

"Yeah...I get what you're saying."

When they entered the house, Katie came running into the living room. It was clear she had a worried look on her face, but the twins didn't say anything.

"Oh...hey guys," she said to both of them. "Sorry, I thought you were your brother."

"You haven't heard from him?" Autumn asked in a worried voice.

"No. I mean, yes. He came back and then headed over to Pete's place. When I heard the door open, I thought maybe it was him...sorry. Just nervous is all," Katie stammered.

Junior shook his head and then walked into the kitchen, looking for something to eat. Autumn stayed with Katie, who clearly needed someone to be with her. Katie's eyes began to glaze over as she sat down on the couch. Autumn exhaled deeply with sadness as she walked over and sat down next to her. Katie wiped the tears out of her eyes as Autumn put her arm around her.

"I'm sorry...I'm just really worried about him," Katie said before she began to cry.

Autumn held Katie tight, trying to make her feel safe.

"It's okay...listen. Garrett going to see Pete is probably the best thing for him. You know better than anyone that he never talks about his emotions. But he does talk to Pete from time to time...and if anyone can get him to talk, it's Pete," Autumn said, hoping to make her feel better.

"I hope so. I don't like knowing that he's in pain. He's just so tough to read; I don't know what he's feeling half the time as it is."

Autumn nodded her head, agreeing. The only way she could tell Garrett was upset or up to something was by looking in his eyes.

"And you know, I never even met Matt. I have no idea what he sounded like or what kind of person he was, aside from the fact that he was funny..." Katie said.

Autumn shook her head as she looked back at some of the moments when she was with Matt, but she didn't want to get into too much detail with Katie.

"He really was funny. He could make anyone laugh, especially Garrett. Some of the stories he's told me sounded interesting. There's no denying they were best friends," Autumn said.

Katie briefly smiled. "Think he'll ever tell me any of those stories?"

Autumn thought about it for a moment. A part of her told herself that he would tell her some of the stories...but not all of them—at least not for a while anyway. But it wasn't her place to say that.

"Yeah, I think he'll tell you...eventually," Autumn said.

Katie shook her head. "I hope so...I would love to hear them and find out more about Matt. I really would."

Autumn patted Katie on the back, showing her support. But inside, Autumn was feeling nauseous despite not being positive about what was going on. She knew it wasn't the time or place to think about that; that time would come eventually. In that moment it was just about trying to be supportive for everyone. The talk about Matt was starting to get to her though, and she knew that the time for her to start accepting he was gone was approaching faster than she had hoped for.

II

By the time Garrett reached Pete's apartment, the sky had broken free from most of the clouds. The Sun had begun to set for the day. He pulled up to the apartment building, parked his truck and got out. He looked up and saw the clouds above him were a beautiful pink and orange, spreading over the city. It was a refreshing sight, for sure, but he only thought about it briefly; there were much bigger things on his mind at that moment.

Garrett locked his truck and headed to the back staircase of the three story apartment building. Climbing up the stairs, Garrett started to think about all the moments and memories he had from living at the apartment with Pete. Moments that made him laugh, moments that made him feel comfortable...and moments with Matt, when he would come over. As he got closer to the top, Garrett knew it wasn't going to be an easy visit like it normally would be for him.

When he got to the top of the stairs and onto the balcony that led into Pete's apartment he got ready to knock. But before he did, he turned and saw Pete sitting in one of the metal chairs he had out on the balcony, just looking out at the view of the city. Garrett slowly lowered his hand from the door and walked over to Pete as Pete finished up his beer. Once Garrett reached Pete, he pulled up a metal chair and then sat next to him. Pete grabbed another beer from the cooler beside him.

At first neither one said anything, they just focused on the view of the city. Both knew they would have to talk, but at that point, just having each other's company was enough for both of them. But when Pete finally broke the silence between the two of them with a sudden laugh, it took Garrett by surprise. It wasn't some weak chuckle either, the laugh came straight from the gut and began turning Pete's face bright red. The sight made Garrett smile too before he broke into laughter also. Pete was laughing so hard, he damn near spilled his beer all over himself and the balcony.

Garrett wiped the tears of laughter from his eyes as he continued to giggle. Both of them knew it wasn't the time to laugh, but in that moment it felt right and it lasted for a long time too. A good five minutes passed before they finally calmed themselves down and got their breathing back to normal.

"I was thinking about the time when we took him fishing. He cast his rod, got it stuck in a tree and when he went to untangle it, he slipped and fell in the river," Pete said with a smile as he shook his head.

Garrett smiled.

"I was thinking about when he picked me up in a snowstorm. He took too wide of a turn when he pulled into his driveway and crashed into the snowbank at the end," Garrett said, chuckling under his breath.

Pete smiled and looked back at the view.

"Fucking Matt, man..." Pete said, like he always would when Matt did something funny/dumb. The smile though quickly disappeared when the harsh reality of what had happened returned to his mind.

"Damn..." Pete softly said under his breath after swallowing another mouthful of beer.

Garrett's eyes began to fill up again, only for a much different reason than last time. Garrett quickly dropped his head and wiped them just as Pete finished up his beer.

"You must be a wreck," Pete said as he cracked open another can of beer.

"I told Mum and everyone I'm fine..."

"Yeah, well, try telling me that you're fine," Pete quickly shot back.

Garrett looked away, his face frozen as he tried to actually tell Pete he was fine...but he couldn't...because he wasn't fine, nothing was fine and Pete knew that better than anyone. Instead of lying to Pete, he chose to remain silent. Pete couldn't, though.

"I don't know what hurts more: the fact that he's gone, or how he chose to leave..." Pete said as he felt tears filling up in his eyes.

The tears in Garrett's eyes began running down his face as he thought of Matt during the last moments of his life and how scared, confused...and lost he was.

"Kid was something special, I just wish I knew what was going on inside...I really do...wish I would've known...and it was right there the whole time too," Pete regretted.

Pete's words sank into Garrett like a lost ship at sea, the words only making the moment harder for him, but deep down he would much rather be with Pete than be alone to deal with his emotions letting loose.

"Pete...?" Garrett asked softly.

Pete cleared his throat after sniffling and then looked at Garrett.

"Yeah?"

"Is it my fault?"

"What?" Pete quickly asked as he turned all the way to him.

"Is it my fault? Did I miss something...?"

"Why would you think that Garrett?"

Garrett swallowed hard as he wiped his eyes. "Because I was his friend. We saw each other all the goddamn time. I saw how happy he always was...how much he made everyone happy...and for the life of me, Pete, I just can't wrap my head around the fact that he...he...I just can't. No matter how much I try," Garrett said, his voice breaking at the end.

Pete inhaled deeply. "I can't either, been trying to figure out why ever since I found out. But I know one thing: you made him happy. I saw that in his eyes every time he was over. You were probably the only thing that made him happy in his life. So don't ever think it was you because it wasn't,"

Pete said, forcing out a smile.

Garrett took in the words and attempted to smile, but the smile didn't stand a chance. The emotions inside gave way, sending tears rushing into Garrett's eyes. And as soon as Pete saw the tears, he quickly turned his chair and put his arms around Garrett.

"I miss him Pete," Garrett said as he sobbed into Pete's shoulder.

"I know buddy..." Pete said, and patted Garrett on the back of the head.

Garrett began to sob even harder.

"It's okay...let it all out."

"I just wanna know why," Garrett said as he sniffled.

Pete didn't say anything, but he wished the same thing. Despite what Garrett said, there was still a small part of Pete that believed Garrett knew more, but just didn't realize he did. When he did figure it out though, Pete knew Garrett was going to be a wreck then, too. But Pete tried to focus on what was before him: a broken-hearted young man who felt so lost, it was difficult to watch. And while Pete held Garrett and they cried in each other's arms, inside Pete's apartment Erin was sitting on the bed and also sobbing, thinking about all the fun moments and laughs she and Matt shared together in the couple of months they had gotten to know each other.

III: Secrets

A round seven in the evening, Autumn started to worry about whether Garrett was with Pete or not. She had sent Pete a text message, asking if he could text her when Garrett leaves but she still hadn't heard anything. The only person who was texting her was Katie, who was at work, asking if Garrett was back yet. After the fourth text message Autumn stopped responding. Like Garrett, she also needed distance to process everything. But unlike him, Autumn was a lot better when it came to dealing with issues, especially major issues. But this was an issue that she had never dealt with before and she knew it was going to be tough this time.

It wouldn't be until around seven-thirty when her phone began to ring. Autumn quickly lifted herself from the couch and answered the phone as fast as she could so it wouldn't wake up Pam. She looked at the screen and saw it was Pete, and let out a huge sigh of relief.

"Pete, thank God. I was starting to get worried."

"Yeah. Just got your text. Sorry it took so long for me to

get back to you."

"Its fine, I was just worried."

"Yeah I'm sure. Anyway he left about twenty minutes ago, so I would assume he'll be home anytime now," Pete said.

"Okay. How is he?"

"Like you would expect. It's tough for him; hell it's tough for all of us but clearly worse for him, at least that's what I'm assuming," Pete confessed.

"I'm sure it is. Listen, can I ask you something?" Autumn asked.

"Yeah."

"Did he say anything...to you about Matt?"

"He said he missed him and wants to know why Matt chose to do what he did. Can't say I blame him there," Pete said.

"Yeah. Did he say anything else?"

Pete got confused.

"What do you mean?"

Autumn exhaled softly, knowing she didn't want to bring it up, but had to in order to find out just how heartbroken Garrett really was.

"You know what I mean, Pete."

Pete didn't say anything at first; he wasn't sure if he should. A part of him felt a bit of relief knowing that it wasn't just him who had a feeling, but no matter what he felt inside, it wasn't his place to say anything.

"No...no he didn't," Pete said, cryptically.

Autumn shook her head.

"Damn it. Well, what do you think Pete? You've spent more time with him than anyone else," she asked, desperately searching for an answer.

"Not going to lie, Autumn, I'm not sure. He's always been hard to read...and this time is no exception," Pete said.

Her eyes began to water as she thought about it being true, not because she was upset about it, but because she knew Garrett was probably in more pain than anyone really thought.

"You think I should ask?" Autumn asked.

Pete exhaled as he thought about whether or not it was a good idea.

"I don't know autumn; he's your brother so maybe he'll feel comfortable talking to you. He might open up to you, he might not. Just keep your guard up," Pete said.

Autumn wiped a few tears from her light brown eyes.

"I just don't get why he's so goddamn stubborn," she said with frustration.

"Well look where he is. He's got a lot to lose right now. I don't agree with how he handled this, but I understand why he did," Pete said.

Autumn agreed, she just wished she could do something for Garrett, something that made him feel safe to talk for once.

"But who knows, maybe I'm wrong. Maybe we're both wrong," Pete shot back with pure uncertainty.

"You really think that?" Autumn asked, a hint of sarcasm in her voice.

Pete shrugged his shoulders. "Right now, I don't know what to think. And I'm sure Garrett feels the same way, so before you start asking, just be prepared for whatever could come after..." Pete warned, remembering how Garrett can be when he feels like he's being backed into a corner.

Autumn exhaled deeply. "I will."

"Okay. We'll I'm going to try and get some sleep."

"Okay."

"So have a good night and just keep an eye on him when he gets in, alright?" Pete asked.

"I will. You have a good night too, Pete."

As she hung up, she couldn't help but replay what Pete had said. Her eyes began to water up again when she thought about all the times when Garrett had been there for her when she was upset or scared, and to think he felt the same way broke her heart. She'd always wanted to return the favor for him at some point; she was just hoping to do it under much different circumstances.

So many ideas were running through her head; so many questions, and it all became overwhelming in that moment. With Pam already asleep, Junior in his room playing video games, and Pete clearly dealing with his own issues, the only person Autumn knew that would be able to help her was Garrett and the moment his truck pulled up to the house, before he even had the chance to put the vehicle in park, Autumn quickly opened the passenger door and jumped in.

"What are you doing?" Garrett asked with confusion and aggravation in his voice.

"Take me somewhere," Autumn said as she closed the

door.

"What? Take you where?"

"Anywhere, as long as we're not here."

Garrett exhaled.

"Autumn, it's getting late and I got work in the morning, I'm not in the mood," he confessed as he put the truck in park and then shut off the engine.

"Garrett, we're going for a ride and you and I are going to vent," Autumn said, firmly.

"Some other time." He opened his door and got out.

Autumn knew she needed to be there for Garrett in that moment and needed to show him tough love in order to get him to talk, but she also knew she was entering that area that Pete warned her about.

"I know you know..." Autumn shouted just as Garrett shut the door.

The slam of the door took most of what Autumn said, but Garrett was able to make out a small fraction of it, which quickly made him reopen the door.

"What did you say?" Garrett asked.

"I said I know."

Garrett looked into her eyes as he leaned in.

"You know what?" Garrett asked. But before Autumn was able to finally tell Garrett what she thought was going on, she looked deep into his eyes and saw the great pain there. And the last thing she wanted was to give Garrett anymore to worry about.

"He was my friend too, Garrett. I mean, I know he was your friend and all but he became mine along the way too," she said.

Garrett shook his head as he lowered it, exhaling deeply as he started to get a headache.

"I know and I'm sorry. It's just...it's not easy okay?"

Silence entered the truck and surrounded them as the sun got lower. Even though Garrett wasn't looking at her, Autumn could clearly tell that Garrett was struggling to stay afloat. Matt's death was doing a number on him, and despite knowing that she couldn't shield Garrett from the pain forever, she wanted to make the moment a little easier for him.

"How about we head down to the lake? Maybe pick up an ice cream at Blake's?" Autumn asked.

"No, told you Autumn I'm tired. I just wanna go in and relax for the night. Not in the mood to drive anyway," he barked.

"How about I drive then? Come on, it'll get you out of the house and we'll get to spend some time together."

Despite not wanting to at first, the idea slowly began to grow on Garrett. He had always enjoyed spending time with Autumn when they both were younger, but growing up had slowly pushed them apart, so he decided to change that for once. He cleared his throat and handed Autumn the keys to his truck.

II

Garrett kept his eyes out the window of the truck as he finished the last bite of his ice cream cone while Autumn took the first bite into hers. She looked at Garrett briefly before putting her eyes back to the road.

"Even to this very day, I'm amazed as to how fast you eat ice cream. I mean, do you even taste it?" She asked with a chuckle.

"I taste the cone every now and then," Garrett said with a

slight smile.

"Haven't had an ice cream from there in so long, I kinda forgot just how good they are," she said before taking another bite.

Garrett turned back to the window as Autumn drove the truck into the dirt parking lot of the lake. Both of them were surprised how many cars and trucks were still there, but not as surprised as when they saw how many boats were still sailing out in the large lake.

Most of the lake was out of the sunlight for the day, but the far back end still held onto it, which was where most of the boats were, trying to get those last few minutes in the spotlight before darkness took over.

"Place is still busy, surprisingly," Autumn said.

Garrett nodded his head gently as he looked around.

"We can park and then I can bring you up to where we go fishing," he said.

Autumn took another huge bite out of her cone as she parked the truck at the end of the dirt lot, making sure it was far enough away from any other vehicles. When she parked, she shut the truck off and put the last of her cone in her mouth and began chewing as she handed Garrett the keys. "Thanks for letting me eat in here."

"Well if I find any crumbs in here later, you won't be thanking me," Garrett said as he opened his door.

Autumn chuckled as she got out of the truck.

"Oh, you'd still love me even if you found a horse head in the back. Course if it was Junior, it would be a different story."

Once Garrett closed his door and he heard Autumn close the driver door, he locked the truck and then looked over to the wooded area just past the lot.

"So, which way do you go?" Autumn asked as she walked over to Garrett.

He pointed. "We normally head in through there."

"Okay, I'll follow you, since I clearly have no idea where the hell I'm going."

"Okay but watch your step, there's poison ivy everywhere. Matt learned that the hard way the first time we went up here," Garrett warned as he began to walk toward the woods.

Autumn started to follow, but then quickly stopped once the words about the poison ivy sank in.

"Whoa, wait a second...did you say poison ivy?"

"Yep. Lots of it."

"And there's no other way to get up there?"

"Nope."

"Well, why do you fish up there, then? There's no better place to catch a fish?"

"I'm sure there is, but I don't go up there for the fish. I go up there for the view," Garrett responded.

"The view? What view is worth walking through a shitload of poison ivy?"

Garrett smiled, remembering Matt asking the same thing to him when he first went up there.

"You'll see."

Autumn shook her head as she watched Garrett step into the woods with no hesitation whatsoever. And when the time came for her to enter the words, she did the exact same thing as her brother, quickly identifying the poison ivy right away as she did her best to keep up with Garrett.

"Shit, you weren't joking. It's all over the place," she said, moving her head left to right over and over.

"Yeah it's always been like this. Ever since I started coming here, anyway. One thing I've noticed though is that it's not too buggy for being in the woods. Nothing like being outside at Mom's anyway."

Autumn groaned with disgust.

"Our backyard is a goddamn nightmare," Autumn said as she ducked under a low tree branch.

"Since when did you start swearing so much?" Garrett asked with a smile.

"Ever since I grew up and realized what our parents were. Nothing's worse than living with an alcoholic."

Garrett lost his smile as he continued up the trail. When his father left when he was around four, he took it hard, nothing's worse than being abandoedn by your own father, and Garrett learned that the hard way. But when Pam met Dave, Dave stepped into the role of being Garrett's father and they formed a strong bond. Dave treated Garrett as if he was his own.

Nothing could change the way Garrett felt about him, he was the only role model he ever had in life, but the tough thing about Dave was that he liked to drink...a lot. Something else Garrett learned the hard way at a young age.

Dave never gets angry when he drinks, but he makes bad

decisions. From gambling at the bar he hangs out at, to spending damn near his whole paycheck on large amounts of liquor. Garrett's known about Dave's problem for a while and he knew it was just a matter of time before the twins started to pick up on it.

The two remained silent for most of the rest of the way up, until Autumn had to stop and take a break from the long walk. Garrett didn't notice she had stopped until he turned and looked all the way back down from the top of the hill he had sprinted up.

"What's wrong?" Garrett shouted down to Autumn.

"It's a long ass walk, that's what's wrong."

Garrett smiled.

"You're echoing Matt today, for sure, he said that too."

"Well can't say as if I blame him...better be one hell of a view, that's all I'm going to say."

III

Autumn complained for pretty much the rest of the hike through the woods, but once they emerged onto a rock ledge that overlooked the entire lake, she quickly stopped as the beautiful view of the boats, the slowly setting sunlight, and the distant mountains took her breath away. She stood in awe. Autumn's reaction brought a smile to Garrett's face as he thought about how it mimicked Matt's reaction the first time he saw it.

"It's beautiful," Autumn said as she looked around.

"I told you it would be," Garrett replied as he walked over to her.

Autumn took her eyes off of the horizon and looked down into the lake. It looked like a mirror as it perfectly reflected the sky.

"How did you find this place?"

Garrett inhaled deeply, taking in the late summer air.

"Needed to clear my head one night. I drove here, saw the trail while I was parked back down in the lot, so I decided to walk it. Never thought it would lead me to something like this. Guess that's how life works sometimes."

Autumn lifted her head up and looked at her brother

"What did you need to clear your head about?" She asked.

Garrett broke eye contact with her and then looked back out at the lake.

"Nothing...it was a long time ago anyway."

Autumn nodded and turned her eyes back out to the lake. "Did Matt like it out here?"

Garrett nodded.

"Yeah, he loved it. He probably spent an hour in the very same spot you're standing, just looking out at the water. Had to check on him to make sure he was okay a couple times actually," he said with a smile.

Autumn chuckled as she thought about Matt looking out at the view. "How did the two of you meet?"

"Met in high school. Freshman year in science class."

"You guy's lab partners together or something?" Autumn asked.

Garrett smiled. "No...he always carried gum, so I would always ask and he would always give me a piece."

Autumn turned and looked at him. "Really? That's how you two met?"

"Pretty much. We didn't talk a whole lot in freshman year, though. It was sophomore year that we really got to know each other."

"Why did you wait until sophomore year?"

Garrett shrugged his shoulders. "A lot was going on at home. Between Mom and Dave splitting up, and taking care of you and Junior while Mom went off and did whatever the hell she did, I guess I was just busy...too busy to see what was in front of me."

"But you did eventually, right?" She asked, keeping her eyes on the boats far out on the lake.

"Did I eventually what?" Garrett asked.

"Eventually saw what was right in front of you?"

Garrett sighed. "I did...but I never treated it the way I should've. I missed out. You know they say the worse thing in life is giving up, but it's not. The worse thing in life is not even starting in the first place," Garrett said with a heavy heart as he sat down on a large rock.

Autumn closed her eyes for a moment, trying to stop the tears from running down her face as the wind softly picked up from behind.

"I remember when I first met him. I think you guys were juniors in high school that year...yeah because we were celebrating your seventeenth birthday. He showed up and spent a good hour with everyone before you and your girlfriend at the time came back. When we heard you coming up the stairs, we all tried to find good places to hide. And sure enough he chose to hide in the trash barrel and I couldn't stop laughing. Thought my laughing might ruin the surprise, but I stopped literally right before you walked in the apartment." Autumn turned and looked at Garrett. "And I'll never forget the look on your face when he popped out of the barrel. You got the biggest smile when you saw him. I was young back then, didn't understand a whole lot about friendship, but that night was the first time I had a feeling...and as the years passed and I got to spend time with you and him and I saw how you two acted and joked around each other...I knew."

Garrett quickly lost the little smile on his face and then looked up at Autumn. His heart began to pound in his chest heavily as tears ran down Autumn's cheek.

"Looking back now, it was obvious, but you hid it well. So did he, now that I think about it, but now I understand why no one would ever suspect anything. Maybe you're not the only one who didn't see what was right in front of them..."

Garrett sat motionless, contemplating what he was going

to say, or if he was even going to say anything at all.

"I don't expect you to say anything; I know you well enough to know that. I'm not going to give you some long speech or force you to let me in and even though I have so many questions that begin with 'why'...I'm not going to ask. I just want you to know that I'm here for you," she said as she walked over and sat down next to him.

Garrett lifted his head when Autumn put her arm around him. Inside he wanted to give her a hug and confess everything for once, but his pride just wouldn't let him. The secrets were still too deep and too meaningful to just let out.

"I love you Garrett. And I know he did too."

Garrett smiled, trying to hold back tears as he looked out at the view, thinking about everything—from how Autumn had just made him feel—to the final words Matt had said to him the last time they saw each other.

'I'll be waiting for you...like I always have.'

As the words replayed over and over in his mind, Garrett could no longer hold back the tears. He lowered his head and tried to hide the pain, and his watery eyes, by burying his head in his arm. But it didn't work, Autumn saw the pain and put her arms around him and hugged him while the distant sunlight left the last part of the lake, symbolizing that one of the last summer nights of the year was getting ready to close in...beginning what was sure to be a long night.

IV: Sunset

Autumn and Garrett spent a while looking out at the lake together once Garrett was able to get his tears under control. Not much else was said between them for the rest of the time they were there; even less was said on the ride back.

"Thanks for the ice cream," Garrett said.

"Thank you for taking me out to the lake. I really enjoyed it," Autumn said with a smile as she ran over another pothole.

Garrett smiled. "Me too."

Autumn was going to add more to the conversation but in the end she decided to remain silent and give Garrett some quiet time, since he wouldn't be able to get that much alone time. The only thing she did for the rest of the ride was look over at him every now and then.

When they reached home, Autumn turned down the dirt driveway and followed it up to the house. As she slowed down to figure out where she was going to park the truck, Garrett moved his eyes away from the passenger window and looked up.

"You can park it right in the front," he said.

"You sure?"

"Yeah, I'll be the first to leave tomorrow morning anyway, so it'll be fine."

Autumn took a wide turn and parked behind Pam's car. Once she put it in park, she turned off the engine and moved the driver's seat back to where it was when she got in. Garrett smiled as he watched her.

"I still can't believe you drive that close to the steering wheel," he said with a chuckle.

Autumn looked at him. "I don't understand how you can drive so far back. I can barely reach the pedals."

"You're just as tall as me!" Garrett said.

"Oh whatever, that's just how I drive I guess. Least I got us home safe," she laughed and shrugged her shoulders. "What time is Katie coming home?"

"Around eleven, I think," Garrett said, opening the door and getting out of the truck.

Autumn closed the driver's door and locked the truck. "You going to wait up for her?"

Garrett shook his head.

"Probably not, I'm wiped out. I need to sleep. Or at least try to sleep."

"Yeah. I think we all do," Autumn said as she got to the front door to the house and unlocked it.

The house was completely dark, meaning Junior had shut off the lights before he went to bed. Once Autumn got in, Garrett followed, closed the door, and realized the same time Autumn did how dark it was in the house.

"Guess I should've told Junior I was going out," Autumn whispered in the darkness.

"Is Mom already sleeping?" Garrett asked as he took out his phone and turned on the bright screen.

"Yeah, she was in bed before we left."

Garrett's large cell phone screen wasn't much of a flashlight in the house of darkness, but between that and the last remaining daylight coming in through the windows, it was just enough to get the both of them to the other side of the room without tripping over anything. They didn't say it out loud, but it was clear the house needed to be cleaned out.

The smell of Pam's cooking got stronger as they reached

the kitchen, but since Autumn's bedroom was just before the entrance to the kitchen, she didn't go any further, despite the smell making her hungry. She reached her bedroom door and turned around to Garrett.

"Alright, I'm going to try and get some sleep," she said as she reached up the wall and turned on the bedroom light.

"Okay. I'll see you in the morning?"

"Maybe. I might attempt to sleep in. Not sure how that's going to work, but we'll find out in the morning I guess," she said with a forced smile.

"Alright, well if I don't see you, then have a good day tomorrow," he said before leaning in and giving her a hug.

"You too, but I'm sure I'll see you..."

Garrett smiled as he noticed both hurt and love in Autumn's eyes.

"You sure you're going to be okay tonight?" She asked.

Garrett tried to keep the faded smile on his face. "I'll be fine."

"Okay, but just promise me you'll wake me up if you need anything."

"I promise."

"Alright then, have a good night Gar Bear."

"You too, sis," he said before slowly letting her go.

Autumn smiled and then walked into her bedroom. Garrett entered the dark kitchen and headed towards his room. Before Autumn closed her door, so the tears could finally give way, she watched Garrett as he made his way into the kitchen and then over to his door, hoping that the time they spent together would be enough to at least blunt the pain, since it was clear pretty much nothing could stop it.

II

Garrett flipped the light switch to the bedroom just as he heard Autumn's door close. Before he entered the room, he took another look around and heard nothing but silence. He was finally alone with nothing but his thoughts, which frightened him the most.

The bedroom was messy, clothes were scattered everywhere, mostly Katie's but some of his were mixed in too. Once he got to the large dresser at the far end of the bed he emptied out his pockets, dropping his truck keys, loose change, and wallet before he started to take off his work boots.

Normally, he wouldn't head to bed until ten or eleven, but all he could think about was taking off his clothes and getting into bed as fast as he could. He was exhausted. When his boots were off, he took off his shirt and then pants before walking over to the queen sized bed. Once he got himself under the warm covers he picked his cell phone up and began typing Katie a text message.

'Heading to bed baby cakes. Sorry I can't stay up for ya but wake me when you get home so I can give you a kiss. Love you baby...now and always...'

As he typed the last words of his message, a flutter went through his chest. It was a strong, instant flutter that started deep in his chest and quickly expanded out and through his whole body...almost the exact same way it did when he was told those three words. And that so ever brief thought of Matt opened the door Garrett was trying so hard to keep closed. But before he knew it, he was suddenly getting out of his text messages and opening up his pictures.

The last picture taken was both him and Katie in a selfie. Both of them looked happy, especially Katie who looked like she was glowing inside and out. The picture brought a slight grin onto Garrett's face just before he slid his thumb to the right. The next one was also with Katie...along with the next and the next.

He never noticed it until then but he had clearly been spending a lot of time with Katie, which made sense since they were together but it wasn't until about twenty pictures into his camera roll that he finally reached a photo of Matt. And as soon as he reached it, he quickly took his hand off of his screen, along with his eyes briefly. He knew memory lane was going to be tough but he also knew it could be just as joyful as it could be painful, which he kept telling himself as he slowly moved his eyes back to the screen.

The photo was taken back in late May, a little over four months before his death. Just by looking at the picture, you wouldn't know anything was wrong; the smile on his face was priceless. Garrett even softly chuckled for a moment as he focused on Matt's face, remembering everything the two of them did on that particular day.

Around mid-May, just as the summer began to really take off, the two of them got the idea to buy two kayaks so they could fish out in the river just down the street from Uncle Pete's apartment. At first Garrett wasn't really on board with the whole idea, it was Matt that ultimately talked him into it and once Garrett finally gave in, they went to pick the kayaks up that same day.

As they drove to the store, both of them were looking forward to going out on the river. Garrett hadn't been out there for a while and Matt had never gone, so Garrett knew it was going to be an interesting adventure just from that fact alone. Everything was interesting when Matt had never done it before.

The both of them were so focused on going out on the river, they didn't even consider the fact that the kayaks were huge...and the car they had wasn't. But they would eventually realize that once they bought them and returned to the car.

"Oh, shit!" Matt suddenly shouted, stopping in the middle of the parking lot.

"What??" Garrett asked in a panic as he turned around with his large green kayak underneath his arm.

"How the Christ are we supposed to get these into the car?"

Garrett also stopped right in the middle of the parking lot, causing several cars to honk their horns.

"Oh shit!" Garrett said.

"Yeah, oh shit."

Before the two of them decided on anything, they had to at least get back to the car instead of just standing in the parking lot with two kayaks that were ten feet long each. Once they finally got back to Matt's green Mazda 3, they both put the kayaks down and then looked at them.

"Why the fuck didn't we think of this sooner?" Matt shouted out in frustration.

Garrett lifted his eyebrows, also surprised by the predicament they were in. "I have no idea. I honestly didn't even think of it and normally I think of these kind of things when you come up with an idea."

Matt then took his eyes off of his pink kayak and looked up at Garrett.

"And what the hell does that mean exactly?"

Garrett looked back at Matt.

"Exactly what you think it means. Every time you come up with one of these brilliant ideas, it's always me that has to either talk you out of it or figure out a way to make it work when it's clearly not going to," he explained.

"Okay then friend: why the hell didn't you think of this before we bought the damn things?"

Garrett thought on it for a moment and then looked back down at the two kayaks.

"Not going to lie, this one got away from me."

Matt rubbed his forehead as he walked over to the trunk, opening it and then lifting it as much as it could go.

"One might fit in there..." Matt said with uncertainty.

Garrett walked over and stuck his head in the trunk, and much to his surprise, there was a lot more room in it than what he thought.

"The seats in the back go down?" Matt asked.

"Yeah..."

Garrett stood back up and then looked back down at the kayaks before turning and looking back at Matt.

"I think you're right...I think one might fit. It might hit the dashboard but it might fit."

Matt shook his head, briefly sighing with relief.

"Okay. What about the other one?"

"I'm still working on that..."

"You think maybe we should leave one here, drop one off at Pete's and then come back for the other one?"

Garrett quickly shook his head with pure frustration.

"No. It'll waste time and it's already three. Besides, that would mean we'd have to do the same thing when we bring them out on the lake," He said as his eyes moved up from the trunk to the top of the car.

Matt watched Garrett's eyes move up and when they stopped moving, he turned to see what Garrett was looking at, but he wasn't able to figure it out at all.

"What? You're thinking something, I can tell."

"How much money you have left?" Garrett asked.

Matt shrugged his shoulders. "Um...probably three hundred bucks...why?"

Garrett grinned as the possibility of bringing both kayaks home turned into an actual chance. "I think I know how to get both of them home."

"How?"

"We're gonna need some rope."

"Rope?" Matt asked as he turned and started following Garrett back into the store. "Rope for what?"

"You'll see..." Garrett said with a smile.

Matt wanted to ask more questions, but he knew there was no point.

"You know, just for the record: I don't have much faith in this," he shouted as he caught up to Garrett.

"I'll note that in the log."

Matt shook his head. "Smart ass."

Garrett turned to Matt and when he saw the disgusted look plastered on Matt's face, he suddenly broke into laughter. Despite having a hard time doing so, Matt was able to keep a straight face. And when Garrett lifted his head back up and saw the same look was still on Matt's face, he patted him on the shoulder.

"Oh, come on bud. It'll be fun. You just gotta trust me."

"Hmm, sure it will be fun."

"That's the spirit. You just have to look on the positive side," Garrett said with all the sarcasm in the world.

"Yeah, coming from the guy that will be in the green kayak

and not a fucking hot pink one."

"You could've chosen purple," Garrett said shrugging his shoulders.

"Shut up," Matt said shaking his head.

III

As Garrett thought of that day, he started to chuckle. Everything from tying down the kayaks and making a huge dent on the fender on the car to getting the kayaks into the river and Matt tipping over, causing him to lose his cell phone in the lake water. As he looked back on those memories, he couldn't help but smile and think it was a good day. He also couldn't help but think that he hadn't thought about that day for a while...or any others recently.

It was in that moment when he realized that in the past month or two, he had become very distant to Matt. Not purposely, he had just become busy with work and Katie. Mostly Katie. Normally he and Matt would talk at least a few times a week before they would hang out during the weekend, but in the final months of Matt's life, those talks quietly disappeared. So did the hanging out on the weekends.

Garrett knew how Matt was; he liked to talk with him. Matt would always say he looked at him like a brother, mostly because Matt came out of the closet to him even before he came out to his own family. Course Garrett never really thought much about that either. He listened, but never fully understood how big of a moment that was for Matt...until he was gone.

Garrett laid in his bed for about a half hour, looking out the window and watching the final light of the sun disappear as his mind went through all the moments the two of them had shared. As his mind looked back on almost ten years of friendship, he smiled and chuckled all along the way. But he lost that smile towards the end. His mind came to a complete halt when it came across that final night they shared together more than three weeks ago.

Garrett had avoided that final memory, knowing he was going to have to play detective and figure out if he could find warning signs of any kind, but he knew he was going to have to face it head on...and so he did.

The last time he saw him was on a Friday, the second week

into August. The whole week leading up to Friday seemed a little odd to Garrett. Normally he would get some type of text message from Matt, whether it was a simple hello or a new joke he came up with but that week was quiet. It wouldn't be until Wednesday night of that week that they started talking and it was Garrett that texted first.

'Hey'

'Hey,' Matt sent back almost a half hour later, which also seemed unusual to Garrett considering Matt almost always responded instantly.

'How've you been?'
'Good.'
'Haven't heard from you in a while.'
'Yeah...'
'Would you like to hang out this weekend?'
'Okay,' Matt answered very basically
'You don't seem very enthusiastic about it.'
'I am. Everything is fine, don't worry.'

'Okay. How's Friday?'

'Friday's fine. I'll be out at noon from work.'

'Okay, I'll text you when I'm on my way over.'

'K.'

Looking back, it made sense to him, but three weeks ago, Garrett didn't think much of it. He acknowledged to himself that the conversation felt a little off, but he ended up just brushing it off, telling himself that Matt was probably just having a bad week for whatever reason.

Garrett kept to his word and texted Matt when he was on his way over. It was a little later then Garrett had hoped for but he was sure that Matt wouldn't mind...and he was right. Garrett had a slight smile on his face as he walked down the stairs and into Matt's basement, like he normally did every time he visited, only he never thought it would be the last time.

Those last laughs, smiles and looks nested deep into Garrett's mind as he drifted in and out of consciousness, and just before he fell asleep, a smile grew on his face as a warm feeling took over inside him that made him feel both comfortable and at peace. Feelings he hadn't felt in a while. And just as another memory popped up, Garrett's eyes closed shut.

V: Awakening

Ever since he was little, Garrett had an almost sixth sense when it came to knowing if he was being looked at or watched while he slept. It was like some type of odd feeling that would build up in the lower half of his gut and alert him. It worked every single time. And it was that very same feeling that made him slowly crack open his eyes not long after falling asleep.

"Rise and shine asshole!" The voice said.

The voice (and remark) took Garrett by surprise, causing him to pop open both his eyes and look straight up at the person that was leaning over his bed.

"Boo," Matt said.

Suddenly Garrett screamed at the top of his lungs, causing Matt to also get spooked and scream out loud. Garrett shot up and out of the bed, backing away from Matt but keeping his eyes locked on him. Matt also took a few steps back as he saw Garrett hit his back on the opposite wall. Then as Garrett stopped screaming, Matt gave the famous half smile that he's given for years.

"Okay. Well on that note...hi," Matt said.

Garrett shook his head and then wiped his eyes, trying to make sure he was seeing what he thought he was.

"Holy shit. What the...Matt?" Garrett asked, confused out of his mind.

"It is I," Matt said with a bow and smile across his face.

"But...how?"

Matt quickly put his hands in the air.

"I'll tell you later, but right now we gotta go. Get dressed and meet me outside, we're late."

Garrett hesitated. "Late? Late for what? What is this?"

Matt rolled his eyes before he turned back around and looked at him.

"Hopefully this isn't what the rest of the night is going to be like. Get dressed. I'll be out here..." Matt began before he turned and looked down at Garrett in his brown boxers. "I'd watch, but I don't want you to wake up in a slimy puddle."

"What!?"

Garrett got dressed as quick as he could, putting on his work shorts, black T-shirt and his work boots, then opened his bedroom door, only to find Matt biting down into a large Snickers bar.

"Oh my frickin God, I can't begin to tell you how much I've been dying for one of these bad boys!" Matt said before taking another huge bite and then throwing the wrapper out.

Garrett did his best to try and remain calm. Inside he was scrambling to make sense of what exactly was happening. He knew that Matt would eventually explain, but he wanted to know right that very second.

"Matt, is this for real?" Garrett asked as the both approached the front door.

"Real as it's going to get pal," Matt shot back, licking off the chocolate from his fingers as he opened the door and walked out of the house and into the mild night.

Garrett quickly followed behind Matt with his eyes fixated on him, still trying to grasp the idea that he was right there, standing in front of him. But as Garrett closed the door to the house and turned around, his eyes quickly went from Matt to what was parked in his driveway.

Matt's car, the orange 2016 Dodge Dart, was parked in the driveway and the car couldn't have been more clean looking, just like it always was when Garrett would see it. The car brought back memories for sure, but it brought even more confusion. Garrett heard that Matt's Grandpa had taken the car and put it into his garage to 'savor' it.

Matt walked over to his car and unlocked it. He put his hand on the door handle, but just as he opened the door, he looked back and saw Garrett was still at the front door, standing very still. Matt was starting to get a little annoyed, but he knew it was going to take Garrett a second or two to grasp everything, so he tried to remain calm the best he could.

"You coming?" Matt shouted out.

Garrett took a deep breath, swallowed hard and then headed to the bright car as Matt sat down in the driver's seat and started it up. A loud roar rose up from the exhaust, instantly putting a smile on Garrett's face as he thought about the first time he heard that very same sound. Then he opened the door and got into the passenger seat just like he always did.

As Garrett got in Matt, like always, checked him out as he sat down. Garrett knew that Matt was checking him out, only this time he decided not to say anything. Once Garrett got in, Matt put the car into drive.

"Okay...here we go," he said before suddenly flooring it.

Garrett grasped the door handle as the turbo-charged engine suddenly blasted them to the end of the driveway before Matt turned the steering wheel to the left and onto the road, the back tires ripping out behind them.

As Matt flew down the road, Garrett couldn't help but feel uncomfortable. He had been in the car before when Matt drove like a maniac, but never under the circumstances he was facing now. He tried to figure out, Why Matt would've faked his own death? While Garrett stared at him like a topless stripper, Matt could tell just from the corner of his eye that Garrett was looking at him.

"Okay this whole staring thing is starting to get kinda awkward pal," Matt confessed without taking his eyes off the road.

"Yeah and this whole, you're supposed to be dead thing is kinda awkward," Garrett shot back.

Matt rolled his eyes. "Oh Jesus Christ, forget about that. Focus on right now."

"No, not until you tell me what the hell is going on."

Matt shook his head as he looked up at the sky and saw it was a dark blue, symbolizing that the night had officially begun. A part of him was thrilled that it had started because he knew what the night would bring, but another part of him felt saddened because he also knew what would happen once the night was over.

The two remained silent for about a mile beyond Garrett's place, but eventually Garrett that broke that silence, hoping to at least get a conversation going.

"Where we going?" Garrett asked as Matt pulled onto the main road.

"Dunkin Donuts."

"Why?"

"Cause we need to get some caffeine in you. Don't want you to fall asleep on me halfway through the night. Wow did that sound a little creepy."

As Matt drove towards the Dunkin Donuts near the highway, Garrett looked all around... he started feeling all around the door only to realize that it all felt so real. He stopped questioning if this was a dream or not, because at that point he simply didn't have a clue.

The two remained silent until they pulled into the parking lot. Matt looked as though he was going heading to the drive through, but he quickly changed his mind, suddenly jerking the car the opposite way and into a parking spot when he realized that he had to pee.

"Sorry about that," he said, pressing the button that shut the car off.

Garrett shook his head, almost in aggravation as he looked around.

"You going to tell me what's going on now?" He suddenly shot out.

Matt looked around.

"Well what's going on is, we're pulling into a doughnut shop, you're going to get coffee and I'm going to empty my bladder because if I don't, there's a real chance I might lose my new car smell," Matt said, opening the door and getting out.

Garrett shook his head as he unbuckled his seatbelt as fast

as he could.

"That's not what I mean!" he said as he opened his door and quickly got out of the Dart.

Matt shut his door and looked at Garrett as he walked around the back of the car. "My God, you ask more questions than a defense attorney. Let's just go in and get a coffee so we can go."

Matt turned away, despite knowing the conversation was far from over. He started towards the entrance, but Garrett grabbed him and turned him around, keeping his hands firmly on both of Matt's arms.

"No, I've let you walk away from dozens of conversations before, but you're not going to walk away from this one," Garrett said, standing his ground as he looked into Matt's deep blue eyes.

But as Garrett waited for a response, Matt grabbed his arms and pushed him into the driver side door, Garrett grunting as his back hit the car. Garrett looked down as Matt held onto his arms.

"Okay listen..." Matt said before he let go of Garrett's right arm and looked at his black wristwatch. "We have...just under nine hours to spend together. After this we won't see each other for a very long time, okay? Now you can either spend this time questioning every little thing or you can finally give in, stop wondering and just have fun like we always do, 'cause this is it. This is where the road ends. So how do you wanna spend our final nine?"

Matt kept his hands firmly on Garrett's arm as he watched his words sink in. Then once Garrett broke eye contact, Matt lowered his hands and began walking towards the doughnut shop while Garrett inhaled deeply, Matt's words echoing in his head. Garrett kept his eyes on him, watching as his best friend entered the little building and looked around for the bathroom. There was no doubt that Garrett was confused, but he was also angry. Angry at Matt for causing him so much pain recently. And that was what Garrett had a hard time trying to wrap his head around. But, if it really was going to be the last time he was going to see Matt for whatever reason, he didn't want tension between them. And in that moment Garrett decided to stop thinking and just go with it; he's done it before with Matt so he figured it wouldn't be any more different from all those times.

"Well, I think I know what I'm getting," Matt said to Garrett, quickly popping up on the other side of him as he stood in line.

Garrett turned to look at Matt before he turned his attention back to the menu.

"Well at least you do. I have no idea what I want."

"How could you not know what you want? Don't you stop here every morning on your way to work?" Matt asked.

"Well, yeah..."

"So how is ordering now any different from ordering then?"

Garrett then looked at him.

"Well for starters, I normally don't order an extra-large coffee at nine o'clock at night."

"You do now," Matt said as he stepped up to the counter. "Hi, could I get an extra-large French vanilla extra/extra and an extra-large dark roast ten and ten?"

Garrett looked at Matt.

"I'm sorry, what was that last one?" the old, short women said as she straightened out her bottle-thick glasses.

"Extra-large dark roast, ten and ten...?" Matt repeated.

The lady lifted her eyebrows and then picked up a large Styrofoam cup with her hand.

"Ten and ten, coming up," she said with a chuckle.

A smile grew on Matt's face as he thought about the sweet and yet strong taste. He reflected back to the first time he tried coffee, back in high school...almost ten years ago, which completely amazed him.

"Ten and ten? You do realize you're gonna be squeezing your ass cheeks just after the second sip, right?" Garrett whispered as he leaned in.

"Hey, sometimes you gotta live on the edge. Leap and the net shall appear my friend, don't forget that," Matt pointed in his face before he turned around and grabbed his coffee.

"Well instead of a net, you better pray that a toilet and colored underwear appear instead."

Matt opened the top of his almost white coffee and blew on it as they headed out the door. "Sick bastard, you make it sound like I've shit my pants before. Well let me tell you something friend, I have never shit my pants...recently...or sober."

Matt stood his ground as they made it back to the car and

looked at one another just before getting in. "Okay, fine, it was once but it was a bad night all around, so it technically wasn't my fault..."

Garrett shook his head and then opened the passenger door. "You shit your own pants, and yet it's not your fault? How the hell does that work?"

"A lot stranger things have happened in the world buddy, like that enema I had to give myself for exsample ...that was awful. Talk about being violated."

Garrett lifted his eyebrows in agreement and then closed the door of the Dart. "So...where to now?"

Matt took a large sip of his cream coffee and then started the car, the ambient lighting quickly creating a comfortable glow. Then a big, almost evil looking smile grew on his face. He turned and looked back at Garrett. "Oh don't worry. I have big plans for tonight."

And just as Garrett was about to ask what Matt meant by that, he was suddenly jerked back and slammed into the leather seat as Matt once again put his foot all the way down to the floor and gunned it out of the parking lot, got into the far right lane of the street and headed onto the highway towards the seacoast.

And that was the start of their little journey.

VI: Heading Off

After sneezing and spilling damn near half his coffee all over his shorts, shoes and seat, Matt floored the Dart up to 75 mph while Garrett played around with the radio, quickly scanning through over a hundred satellite radio stations in about two minutes. From heavy metal to classic forties music, he went through them all, trying to find that right tone of music for the ride ahead.

"How about instead of going through all twelve hundred channels again, you find one and stick with it?" Matt asked with annoyance as he took one of the last sips of cream and sugar in his cup.

"Hey, don't get mad at me just because you spilled your creamy coffee all over yourself."

Matt shook his head as he looked down at his speed.

"Thanks for reminding me," he said as he started to move his hips and legs around.

Garrett didn't say anything at first, but he clearly knew what was wrong with Matt: he burnt his balls when he spilled the coffee all over his seat. And Garrett couldn't help but giggle a little at the sight as Matt did his best to try and keep the car in the same lane.

"So, how're your balls doing?" Garrett asked with as much innocence as he could fake.

"One is beyond cooked; I know that for a fact. I mean if it was anymore burnt it would probably turn to ash and fall off," he began as Garrett started laughing. "The other one I think is still there, maybe seared around the edges, but I think he'll make it. Not really sure where he is though, haven't found him yet."

"Well that's good...I think?"

Matt exhaled. "Yeah, guess that information could go either way."

"Little bit, but I'm used to it now."

Matt exhaled softly and then looked back towards the road, while Garrett lifted his head and looked up through the sunroof and into the sky. Once his eyes focused just right, he gasped, amazed as to how clear and bright all the stars were.

Matt turned when he heard Garrett, but once he realized why, he smiled and gave Garrett a few moments to really take it all in.

"How's the view up there?"

"Incredible! I don't think I've ever seen the sky look so clear before," Garrett confessed as he came back down to Earth and took another sip of his coffee. "How in the name of Christ can you drink ten and ten in your coffee? I'm already starting to feel jittery and I only had four sips."

"Can't tell you, that's a secret."

"Kinda like where we're going is a secret?" Garrett quickly shot back.

"I told you where we we're going!"

"No, you didn't!"

Matt took a moment to think and as it turned out he actually wasn't sure if he told Garrett.

"Oh...well I meant to, so the thought was there at least."

"So, where the hell are we heading to?"

"Hampton."

"Beach?"

"No, casino. Of course the beach!" Matt said with sarcasm.

"Okay chill! I was just asking."

"Well, you ask too many questions. You're so busy trying to figure out how life works when you should be busy living it instead of questioning it. Sometimes the best way to see is to stop looking."

"Read that off a bumper sticker, did you?" Garrett responded.

"Yeah, off a purple Toyota Prius, almost as if the car was saying sorry for being such an ugly ass eye sore. Of course driving is probably not the best time to stop looking, but you get my point. Wow, way to ruin the moment, you jerk," Matt ranted.

Garrett laughed. Matt did also but began to feel bad, fearing that Garrett might've thought he was being rude...and he didn't want the night to turn into a fight. There had been quite a few times where they went from laughing and joking, to yelling and then leaving, and each time it made the both of them feel like complete shit. And that wasn't what Matt wanted to have for a last memory together. So instead of letting the moment pass by, Matt seized the opportunity to make it his own.

"Anyway, I know the last time we went to the beach wasn't entirely pleasant..." Matt began.

"You talking about when you ran my truck off the road and into a guard rail or when you threw up in the water next to those two small children?" Garrett smirked.

"Anyway...since the last time wasn't pleasant for either of us, I'm hoping we can make up for that tonight."

"You vomited out scrambled eggs and red Jell-O less than a foot away from a two-year-old child."

Knowing there was no way on Earth he could actually come up with a positive thought that made him come out looking like the good guy, Matt simply went with the first thing that popped up in his head.

"Well, who knows, maybe I saved that kid from a shark attack that day."

"In two inches of water?"

"Maybe it was a baby shark..."

Garrett shook his head, still surprised after all these years as to how fast Matt could come up with something on the spot. Before he knew it, he found himself looking at Matt again as he drove, completely unable to take his eyes off his friend. Garrett couldn't put his finger on it, but he could tell something was different about Matt. He looked the same, he talked the same, but it was almost as if his presence was different. Stronger, bolder, and filled with adventure, just like how he was when they first met all those years ago.

"You're staring at me again, G..." Matt said as he looked from the corner of his eye.

As soon as Matt said that, Garrett quickly pried his eyes away and focused on the dark highway before them.

"Sorry."

A slight smile grew on Matt's face in the ambient lit cabin of the car. "If it makes you feel better, I'm flattered that you're looking at me. Normally you never look at me."

"Oh shut it," Garrett quickly shot back with a chuckle.

Matt also laughed and then ended the conversation by turning up the volume on the radio. Garrett was about to tell him that he was wrong about him never looking, but Matt made it to the radio too quick for him to say it.

The song that came on the radio was none other than one of Garrett's most favorite country songs. Matt, being an average metal fan, always dismissed country (and pretty much every other type of music) and expressed his belief that metal was the only way to go. But much to Garrett's surprise, Matt didn't change the station once they realized what song was playing. Matt even seemed to be enjoying it, bopping his head around during the chorus.

"You feeling all right?" Garrett asked during a quieter part of the song.

"Never better, why?"

"Well it kinda looks like you're enjoying a country song and I don't think I've ever seen you do that before."

Matt shrugged his shoulders and looked back towards the road.

"Well people do change, it's just not always easy to see...and this is actually a rock song too."

"Bullshit!" Garrett quickly responded. "There is no way in hell that this is a rock song. This is pure country music."

Matt smiled. "No it's not."

"Yes, it is!"

"No, it's not and do you wanna know how I know it's a rock song?"

"How?" Garrett quickly asked as he leaned in closer.

"Because I like the song. Therefore, it's not country and your argument is invalid."

"Oh my God!"

"Case in point right there," Matt said with a smile.

"Oh, this is going to be a long ass night."

"That's the spirit!" Matt said with complete excitement in his voice, like that of a five-year-old kid.

Garrett couldn't help but chuckle and looked back out the passenger window, wondering what type of mischief Matt would be getting them into next. As Matt pulled off the highway and onto an exit ramp, a large red sign grabbed Garrett's attention, and he knew instantly what was about to happen next.

"Oh, this is going to be fun..." Garrett muttered.

II

As Matt pulled up to 'Sean's Go Karts of New England' he quickly noticed how busy it was. Garrett noticed it too but wasn't too concerned. Matt pulled into the parking lot and started looking for a spot.

"Let me know if you see an empty spot," Matt said as he looked all around.

As Garrett started looking, he noticed that some of the cars looked familiar...very familiar. The first car he noticed was a silver Dodge Stratus, much like his first car. Next to the Straus was a white Chevy Blazer, like the one he got when his Stratus shit the bed.

"Huh..."

"What?" Matt asked.

"Nothing it's just...nothing," Garrett said, scratching his head in confusion.

"Okay...found one!" Matt shouted out loud.

Garrett looked up and saw a Black Ford truck backing out of a spot right in the front of the parking lot—much like the black Ford truck his former girlfriend let him drive when they were together. Once the truck drove away, Matt spun the wheel and put the car in reverse, turned his head to the back window, and started to slowly back in.

Garrett's attention was taken by the large touch screen on the dash board, showing the backup camera. He turned back to Matt.

"Um, you do realize you have a backup camera, right?"

"Yes I do, smartass, but its okay. I don't need it."

Garrett turned back to the screen and saw that the curb and metal 'Customer Parking Only' sign was getting extremely close to the rear end of the car.

"Okay, you should be good," Garrett said.

"Just a little more."

"No, you're good."

"The car is big."

"Oh Jesus Christ, here we go."

Matt exhaled and turned to Garrett while the car kept going backwards.

"You wanna drive then, if you think you can do such a better job?"

"Sure, just give me the keys. I actually drive good!"

"So do I!" Matt snapped back.

"Oh, that's a load of shit. *I've* never gotten into a crash!"

"Neither have I!"

But just before Garrett could respond with a sarcastic remark, the back tires of the car hit the curb. The car drove up it and then right into the sign, shattering the wooden pole and causing the large metal sign to fall and land on the trunk of the car and back window, cracking the window and leaving huge dents, chipped paint and holes in the trunk before sliding off the car and onto the ground.

Garrett kept his eyes on the screen, watching it all happen through the backup camera, while Matt watched the sign fall through the rear view mirror. Once he heard the sign crash onto the pavement, he slowly looked down at Garrett who had a large smirk across his face.

"See? Perfect," Matt said with a smile before shutting the car off.

Garrett thought about responding, but knew there was no reasoning with Matt. He ultimately decided to simply shrug his shoulders and open his door. They got out of the car.

The two of them started toward the entrance of the park, neither one mentioning what had just happened to the car. As they made their way closer to the entrance, they noticed a lot of people were playing mini golf. The golf course was full of obstacles and a large waterfall in the middle of the course, which grabbed Garrett's attention.

"Holy shit, that's a big course."

"The waterfall is pretty cool."

"Is that why we're here?" Garrett asked.

Matt turned and looked at him as he opened the door to the small shack where tickets are purchased.

"You really think I'd bring you here just so we could play a game of mini gulf?" Matt asked as he walked up to the counter. "Two for the Go-Kart track."

The young Chinese man behind the counter smiled and then started typing into the register.

"Uh yes, two for Go-Kart track."

Matt gave the guy a quick smile just before he looked down at the man's name tag. Matt double-checked to make sure it said what he thought it said: 'Fook'. Matt began to chuckle under his breath. Fook didn't pick up on the laughter but Garrett certainly did.

"What's so funny?" Garrett asked as he leaned in.

Matt then whispered in his ear. "Look at his name tag…"

Garrett took his eyes off of Matt and then looked down at the name tag.

"Fook?" Garrett asked out loud trying to figure out if that's how you pronounce the name.

"Yes?" Fook asked as he looked up from the register.

Garrett looked up. He hadn't expected Fook to say anything, but now that he had, he knew he was going to have to say something so he wouldn't think he was making fun of his name.

"Uh, um..." Garrett stammered.

"How long have you been working here?" Matt quickly asked, taking the attention off Garrett, who sighed in relief.

"Oh, uh almost three years now," Fook said with a smile, before he turned to the printer behind him.

Matt smiled and cleared his throat before Garrett leaned in.

"Thanks."

"Hey..." Matt began, causing Garrett to lean in closer. "I think I know what his last name is..."

Garrett shook his head.

"Oh good God, no..." he said as he turned and walked away.

Matt chuckled and then looked back at Fook, who printed the two tickets, ripped them off the machine and then handed them to Matt with a big smile across his face.

"There you are."

Matt took the tickets with a smile. "Thank you."

"Anything else I can do for you?" Fook asked.

"Yeah, I have a question for ya..."

Garrett's eyes quickly grew wide with fear. He knew what was coming next, he had been in a similar situation before with Matt and he somehow had to shut him up. He quickly turned around and headed back to Matt as fast as he could.

"Your last name wouldn't happen to be Hing, would it?" He asked just before Garrett grabbed him by the hand and pulled him out of the little shack.

"Okay, time to go before you get us killed," Garrett ordered.

"Awe come on, it was just a question."

"Yeah, it always starts with just a question."

As the two headed into the park, Matt brought himself back down to reality by looking down at his watch to see just how much time he had left with Garrett. And just like every other time he would look at his watch, Matt was surprised at how fast time was ticking away.

VII: Full Throttle

Garrett glared at Matt as the two made their way to the Go Kart track. Matt could see Garrett wasn't exactly happy.

"I had to."

"No, you did not have to ask if his name was Fook Hing!"

"You're right...I needed to!" Matt said with an evil chuckle, then he ran toward the Go Kart entrance and up to the front of the gate.

Garrett followed him, smiling at how excited Matt was. The look on Matt's face was a look he hadn't seen for months. Matt smiled every time they hung out, but toward the end, Garrett could see that something was off. But this time it was clear that the smile was genuine, nothing seemed to be hiding behind it, as far as he could tell.

As an older man opened the gate, Matt ran to the front of the line of Go Karts and hopped into a light blue one with a large three painted on the side. Garrett also headed to the front of the line, but slower than Matt as he looked around. He wondered why no one else was at the Go Kart track, but he shrugged it off and walked over to the Go Kart side by side to Matt's. But before he got into it, he stopped; the Kart was a hot pink color.

"Really?"

Matt chuckled and sarcastically put his hand over his cheek to be dramatic. "Oh my...I think your Kart is pink."

Garrett glance at Matt's blue Go Kart. He shook his head and then sat down in the pink Kart, watching Matt grow the biggest and evilest looking smile on his face. But Matt suddenly stopped and groaned in pain as he lowered his hand from the small steering wheel and took hold of his privates.

"Awe, what's wrong?" Garrett asked, feeding Matt some of his own medicine.

"My balls still hurt from the coffee," he confessed.

"Pussy," Garrett quickly shot back as he put on his helmet.

Matt looked up as the old man, Herb, walked past them and stood in front of their Go Karts. When Matt made eye contact with Garrett again, Garrett smiled as Matt exhaled an angry and sinister chuckle.

"Sounds like someone is looking for an ass whooping."

Garrett suddenly laughed out loud.

"Oh, that's good...it's good to start off with a joke," Garrett replied with that same smile on his face.

Matt began to rev his Go Kart. He looked up at Herb. It was obvious just by looking at him that Herb's youthful days had long since passed, between his long white beard and his shorts—so high up they could be mistaken as underwear from a distance. But despite that, the two did attempt to not say anything).

"Okay! Here's the deal!" Herb shouted as loud as he could. "You'll each get five laps around! Do your best to stay on the track, keep your hands inside the Kart at all times and most of all, no bumping into each other!!"

Matt and Garrett's eyes both grew big with fear as he shouted.

"Understand?"

Garrett nodded, while Matt put up his thumb.

"Good! When the light behind me turns green, you're good to go!"

Matt nodded and then Herb walked off the track and over to his little stand. Garrett tightened his helmet. Once he got it tight enough he turned and looked back at Matt. When he saw that Matt was looking at him, he smiled.

"You're going down...punk," Matt growled.

Garrett shook his head.

"You got nothing!" He shouted back and began revving the pink Kart.

The two then took their eyes off of one another and looked at the set of lights. The red light was the only one illuminated, but suddenly it changed to yellow. Matt started to rev his Kart before he smiled and turned back to Garrett. When Garrett saw Matt turn out of the corner of his eye, he turned.

"Watch this!"

And once the light switched over to green, Matt put his foot down hard on his gas pedal, blasting past Garrett. Garrett quickly lost his smile when he saw Matt take off down the track.

"Oh, shit," he cried, before gunning it himself.

As Garrett floored it to catch up with Matt, Herb watched from the security hub and chuckled as he cracked open a beer.

"Kids..."

II

Matt kept a smile on his face for just about the first full lap—turning around a couple of times and seeing that Garrett was having a difficult time trying to catch up—but he quickly lost it when from out of nowhere, Garrett pulled up alongside him.

"Hi buddy!" Garrett shouted.

"Get out of here! Cheater!" Matt shot back.

"How the hell am I cheating? I'm just driving."

"Bullshit."

"This all you got, bud?" Garrett asked as they approached a tunnel.

Garrett's dismissal of the chance that Matt could win sent Matt into competition mode. As they entered into the tunnel, Matt floored it, causing his Go Kart to fly out in front of Garrett.

"Bastard," Garrett said, stomping down on the gas pedal.

Once Matt exited the tunnel, he quickly looked behind him.

"Up yours, pal!" Matt shouted as he lifted his middle finger in the air.

Garrett looked up at Matt's finger flying high before he pushed down harder on the gas. He almost hit the wall from taking the corner so sharply. It was a close call but Garrett just made it and was able to catch back up with Matt, who ended up slowing down for the turn. As Garrett once again pulled up alongside, the two made eye contact just before Matt stuck his tongue out.

"Mines faster!" Matt shouted with pride.

"Mines bigger!" Garrett shot right back, catching Matt off guard and flying past him.

Once he picked his jaw up off the floor of the Go Kart, Matt floored it and was able to catch up to Garrett before they reached the tunnel again, pulling right up alongside him with rage in his eyes.

"Was that a penis reference?!" Matt asked as his eyes bounced between Garrett and the track.

Garrett gave Matt that sinister smile as they approached the tunnel. "Truth hurts, doesn't it?"

"How many times do I have to tell you? I'm a grower, not a shower."

"Hopefully, it's one hell of a growth spurt, then..." Garrett shot back with a smile.

Matt sunk his eyes in Garrett, glaring at him like no tomorrow, in mock anger from what Garrett had said.

"Like I said," added Garrett, "truth hurts, don't it?"

And as it turned out, Matt wasn't very fond of the truth, and with a loud groan he turned the steering wheel to the left and then suddenly jerked it to a hard right, crashing into Garrett's Go Kart, pushing it towards the right and almost into the wall.

"Whoa, what the hell are you doing?" Garrett quickly shouted, losing the smile on his face.

Instead of answering, Matt chuckled and then slammed into Garrett's Kart again, only harder than the first time.

"You trying to get us killed?" Garrett shouted.

"Take it back!" Matt said as Garrett pulled up to his side.

"No!"

Matt shook his head and then crashed into Garrett again, taking out his headlight and a large section of pink paint as they pulled up to the security hub. As the Go Karts got closer, Herb lifted his head up and saw smoke coming from the Karts as they approached. At first he thought it was something serious, but once he realized it was smoke coming from the tires rubbing each other he quickly figured out what was going on.

"Oh, hell no..." he said, before opening the door of the hub and running out onto the course.

"Take it back!" Matt ordered as he crashed into Garrett again.

"No!" Garrett said as he got ready to stoop down to Matt's level and retaliate.

But just before he did, they both looked up and saw Herb standing in front of them on the track with both his hands out.

"Stop! Stop right now!" He ordered with anger.

As they got closer it was obvious to Herb that neither one of them were going to stop, and he quickly jumped out of the way as Matt and Garrett flew past him.

"Little rounded pieces of shits!" Herb muttered, landing on the ground

As they got further down on what was their last lap, Garrett jerked his steering wheel to the left and crashed into Matt, causing his Kart to swerve. Matt weaved to the left but was able to stabilized his Kart before looking up and shooting Garrett an angry look.

"How do you like it?" Garrett asked with sarcasm.

Matt then swerved to the right and crashed back into Garrett, completely stripping away the pink paint as the metal frames of the karts started rubbing together.

"Take it back, asshole!" Matt shouted as he turned his steering wheel to the right.

"Hell no!" Garrett responded, pushing his steering wheel to the left.

Both of them kept their eyes on one another's karts as sparks began flying out until they reached the tunnel. When they entered the tunnel, Garrett focused his eyes on the track. Matt looked down and saw Garrett's kart slowly starting to break away and push in front of him...and he was not about to let that happen.

Garrett smiled when he realized he was starting to get ahead, but the smile didn't last long. Once the two emerged from the tunnel, Matt quickly pulled away from Garrett, causing his front bumper to snap off. When the piece of bumper flew past him, Matt forcefully turned his steering wheel as hard as he could to the right and soared back into Garrett. The impact of the hit caused Garrett's Kart to shoot across the track, taking him by surprise.

"Whoa, what the..."

And before he could finish his sentence, Matt came back over and slammed into Garrett again, causing him to crash into the wall. As he hit the wall, his Kart bounced off it and spun all around before it stopped in the middle of the track, the engine hissing and pouring out smoke as Garrett looked down, shaking off the dizziness from the spins.

"Son of a bitch!"

Matt turned back around and saw Garrett's Kart in the middle of the track, not moving and smoke pouring out of it, which instantly made him smile.

"Can't beat the best, sucker!" Matt shouted as he waved and cheered into the night air.

Matt was so busy laughing and looking back at Garrett, he didn't even see the large black bumper in the middle of the track. He plowed right into it, causing him to shoot up out of the Kart and into the air as the Kart stopped dead in its tracks.

Matt was in the air for a good five seconds before he came back down onto the ground, landing hard on his ass in a patch of grass just outside of the race track. Stars circled around his head.

Silence took over the entire track as smoke poured out of both Karts. Matt was brushing himself off when he heard a loud scraping noise coming from behind him. At first he paid no attention to it, but once the noise got louder and closer, he turned, only to see Garrett slowly pulling up to him with his Kart all mangled and damn near broken. He stopped once he got next to Matt and then looked at him.

"The best, huh?"

Matt briefly chuckled and then looked at Garrett.

"You know what? Why don't you just..." Matt began but stopped when he saw Herb and two security guards walking over to them.

They both looked at another for a moment before Garrett lowered his head, while Matt looked up at all three of them and smiled.

"Kart drives great, if that makes a difference..." Matt said happily, just as fire began to come out of the engine in his Kart.

The two security guards and Herb turned and looked at the Kart, watching the flames coming out of the engine before the little vehicle suddenly blew up, shooting flames and thick smoke up into the night air. Garrett didn't even bother to look at the Kart as it burned behind him; he already knew what was happening. Matt also knew but that didn't stop him from taking a glance. He turned and looked back up at Herb.

"Or *drove,* I guess I should say..." Matt said, keeping his large smile fixed on Herb and the guards.

Garrett shook his head in disbelief just before all four tires under him blew, sending him and his Kart onto the track with a loud bang.

"Awesome..."

VIII: Pure Shores

"**W**ell, that was fun," Matt finally said after a half hour of silence in the car.

Instead of responding vocally, Garrett chose a different approach; turning to Matt and giving him an extremely pissed off look as he wiped off his shirt. When Matt saw the look, he slowly lost his smile and then turned back to the highway.

"So I take it you're still pissed at me..."

"You tried to kill me with a Go Kart," Garrett growled, trying his best to keep his temper under control.

"Well...not at first, but you gotta look on the bright side."

"And what's that? What's the bright side to having you run me into a wall with a Go Kart?"

"It was fun?" he said with a chuckle. "With the exception of the three-thousand-dollar bill for the Go Karts that is."

Garrett rolled his eyes and then turned on the radio. "Where to next, you murderous bastard?"

Matt looked up at the large sign just off the right hand side of the highway.

"Well Hampton Beach is about ten minutes away, you hungry?"

Garrett shrugged his shoulders. "Yeah, I could eat."

Matt nodded. "Good cause I'm taking you to the best pizza place in the world."

Garrett chuckled at the excitement in Matt's voice, something he hadn't heard in a very long time...and it got him thinking about everything again.

"So, we gonna talk about what's going on yet?" Garrett asked.

"Nope," Matt quickly answered. "You like square pizza right?"

Matt's question threw off Garrett for a moment, confusing his train of thought.

"What? Yeah square is fine, when are you going to tell me?"

Matt took his eyes off the road and looked down at the clock.

"Uh, sometime in the next three to five hours."

Garrett exhaled, shaking his head in annoyance. Matt turned and saw Garrett crossing his arms and looking out the window. It was clear that he was going to have to answer *something*; Garrett was getting pissed. With a sigh, Matt took his eyes off of Garrett and looked back out the windshield.

"Remember when you stayed with me for the summer? Must've have been almost five years ago now; you shot me in the ass with a blow dart gun?"

Garrett instantly started to chuckle. "Yeah, I remember that."

"That really hurt, you know."

"You said I could."

"Yeah, but I didn't think you actually would!"

Garrett shrugged his shoulders. "Shit happens, bud."

Silence filled the car for a brief second. "I still have the scar, you know..."

Garrett started to laugh again and then laughed even harder when he remembered back to the look on Matt's face when he turned around and saw the six-inch dart stuck in his left ass cheek.

"Well it was funny, kinda like the time when we went to

that mud truck rally and you slipped and fell in the mud."

"Yeah, that sucked too."

"Aw, come on, we've had a lot of good times."

Matt smiled. "Oh I know, trust me."

Garrett smiled and looked out the window before turning back to Matt. "Why'd you bring that up?"

Matt then turned to him. "To remind you..."

"Remind me of what?"

"What we have. What we'll always have. Even when it feels like we don't have it anymore."

Garrett looked down as Matt's words sunk in deep. He got scared.

"Matt, what the hell is going on?"

"Change...but might as well ignore that while we can."

Garrett still wasn't satisfied with Matt's answer, but it was clear that whatever was going on, it was going to affect more then he originally thought. And despite still wanting about a dozen answers, Garrett couldn't help but agree with Matt about waiting to deal with change when the time came. So even though that time was rapidly approaching, the two of them decided to place it on the back burner as they made their way into the town and beach of Hampton.

II

The engine roared in the orange Dart as Matt pulled up to the main street and turned on to it. They looked around, amazed as to how busy the place was. Garrett checked the clock in the radio.

"Busy for past eleven at night."

"You can say that again. Normally, I would've been sleeping three hours ago," Matt said as he turned and looked toward the water and saw all the people both on the beach and in the ocean.

"Can't complain though, always wanted to come at night. Been told there's quite a nightlife to be seen."

"Yeah, I've always wanted to come too."

Garrett put his hand on his stomach as it began to rumble. "How far is this pizza place of yours?" he asked.

"Not far. Maybe two miles."

"Okay good, cause I'm actually really hungry now."'

Matt smiled and then pushed down on the gas a little

harder. He made his way to the end of the street while Garrett continued to look around at the nightlife of the entire shore. He thought back to the first time he was brought there, by his Mom and her boyfriend at the time. It felt like another lifetime ago in his mind.

"Is it weird that coming here brings back a lot of memories?" Garrett asked.

"Nope, I was thinking the same thing. I remember the first time my grandparents brought me here...doesn't seem like it's been over twenty years already. Life moves fast though, so I guess I shouldn't be so surprised," Matt said as he pulled onto another street when the light turned green.

"Yeah..." Garrett said as he looked up at all the lit up beach houses and saw how close together they were. "I'll never understand that."

"Understand what? Why life goes by so fast?"

"No...well, yeah that too, but I meant building all these beach houses so close together."

Matt turned and looked at them. Pretty much all of them were built side by side. Many of them didn't even have a yard or even much of a driveway.

"Yeah, I know right? You get no privacy and at the beach you want privacy, if you catch my drift."

Garrett smiled.

"Yeah, I know what you mean, course I'm not one to judge. I kinda did 'stuff' in an alley behind my old apartment."

Matt shook his head. "You know that doesn't really surprise me."

"Young and dumb back then I guess," Garrett shrugged his shoulders.

"When was this?" Matt asked, taking his eyes off the street briefly.

"When you came over for my birthday back in high school and we all played Manhunter in the alley behind the apartment building."

"Well, that explains why none of us could find you for like a half hour."

Garrett chuckled while Matt drove onto a long bridge, high above the cold ocean water. About halfway across, they both looked down, amazed as to how calm and beautiful the water looked.

"Always wanted to live around here," Garrett confessed.

"Yeah, nothing like living next to a nuclear power plant," Matt shot back as he pointed towards an oval shaped building across the water.

Garrett turned and looked at the awkwardly designed building. "Well...least it would be quick."

Matt chuckled. "Since when do you start looking on the bright side?"

"Oh shut it and just get us to this damn pizza place."

Matt nodded. "You got it."

Matt lifted up his right foot and then stomped it onto the gas pedal, sending the RPM skyrocketing up to the number seven and causing the car to fly across the rest of the bridge and soar down the street. Matt stayed very focused while Garrett glued his eyes on the digital speedometer, watching it shoot up to sixty.

Matt had a huge smile on his face. It was an incredibly infectious smile, causing Garrett to also smile in an instant. It was clear that the old Matt was back...and Garrett couldn't have been happier about that.

But Garrett's smile faded a bit when he glanced back down and fixed onto the clock in the middle of the touch screen. For the briefest second he didn't think much of it, but when Matt's words of it being the last time they see one another for a while began replaying in his head, he started to add up how many hours they roughly had left, quickly realizing that almost half the night was over and that horrified him. He took his eyes off the clock and put them back on Matt, feeling somewhat sad in the moment. The end was coming at him head on and it was just a matter of hours before he would have to face it.

III

Matt quickly slowed down, squealing the tires as they came to an abrupt halt at a stop sign. Soon as the car stopped, both of them firmly jerked in their seats before Garrett turned and looked at Matt.

"Break much?"

"Sorry," Matt said as he turned left and towards a small plaza.

"Jesus Christ. And you call my driving bad," Garrett mocked, shaking his head.

"It is. I may get us into an accident, but the way you drive, you'd get us into a coma."

"Okay, that's bullshit," Garrett quickly responded.

"Tell that to that stop sign you crashed into back in high school."

"You ran me off the road!"

"I did not! I was in the street long before you were, therefore you should've yielded!"

"Kinda hard to yield when some asshole in an Oldsmobile flies up behind you at a hundred miles an hour!"

Matt rolled his eyes. "Oh my God, it's been seven goddamn years and you still bring this up like it was yesterday."

"Yep," Garrett quickly answered before looking out the windshield. "Where the hell are we?"

"Salisbury."

"Salisbury, Mass?"

"Yes, sir. Why, you've been here before?"

"No, just heard of it."

Once the red light in front of them turned green, Matt drove across the intersection and up to the plaza, looking around for a parking spot.

"See a good place to park?" He asked.

Garrett started looking around and then quickly locked onto a spot right on the end of the street.

"Right there," he pointed.

Matt turned and looked at the spot before starting to question the size of the space. "You think we'll fit?"

"We're in a Dodge Dart not an RV; you should be fine."

"Valid point."

Taking Garrett's advice, Matt turned the wheel towards the spot and began to slowly pull in.

"Am I close to the curb?" Matt asked as he slowly pulled in.

"I can't see, hold on."

As Matt slowed down, Garrett grabbed a hold of the door latch and then opened just as the car drove past a parking meter. Suddenly a loud bang lifted up into the air as Garrett's door shook. Taking Garrett by surprise, he quickly closed the door, only to see the now bent meter slowly passing by. His eyes quickly grew big with fear.

"Shit."

"What was that noise?" Matt asked as he shut the radio off.

Knowing how Matt would react, since clearly there would

be a dent, Garrett took a moment to answer. He thought about telling the truth but then decided he wanted to keep Matt in a good mood for the rest of the night.

"I didn't hear anything," he said with a big smile on his face.

Matt looked confused for a second, trying to figure out what the sound could've been but in the end he just shrugged his shoulders.

"Huh...must be losing it," he said as he shut the car off and then opened the door.

Garrett briefly chuckled and once Matt got out of the car and closed his door, Garrett lost his smile and quickly grabbed the latch of his door again. "Shit, shit, shit."

Hoping for the best, Garrett slowly opened the door and took a deep breath. Once he got his feet out, he turned and looked at the bent meter. He shook his head in disbelief and then very slowly looked toward the bottom of the meter, only to see the front side of the metal pole had marks of orange on it. When his eyes noticed the orange, he got up out of the car and closed the door to look at it, only to have his jaw drop to the ground.

The door looked like the right hand side of the Titanic: large gashes, indents, and missing paint covered the entire lower half of the door. Garrett couldn't believe his eyes and he knew Matt would flip if and when he saw it.

"Oh shit," he shouted, grabbing Matt's attention from across the car.

"What?" Matt asked as he stopped and turned around.

Garrett quickly lifted his jaw off the ground, looked up at Matt and smiled.

"Nothing, just amazed by the place," Garrett lied through his teeth before starting to look around at all the little shops and pizza places.

Matt smiled and started to look around himself.

"Yeah...it's pretty nice around here. Very quiet compared to Hampton. Come on, I'll show you around."

Garrett shook his head.

"Great, sounds good." He carefully closed the door, looking down at the huge mark one last time.

He ran around the front of the car and over to Matt as Matt started walking toward the sound of what seemed to be waves. Just before they made it to the beach, Garrett lifted his eyes up to Matt and noticed he looked very tired.

"Everything alright?" he asked.

Matt turned and looked at him. "Yeah, why?"

Garrett nodded. "You just look a little sluggish all of a sudden."

"Yeah, just tired is all. Driving does that to me for some weird reason."

"I get like that too. Sucks getting older."

Matt smiled before looking up at the large full moon in the brilliant night sky. "Beautiful."

Garrett looked up and was suddenly taken by just how amazing the sky looked. He had never seen the sky look so clear and healthy looking. Everything about it looked perfect.

"Shit, wow. Looks like something out of a painting."

"Or a Mac wallpaper."

Garrett chuckled.

"Yeah...that too."

When he looked at Matt, his smile quickly went away once he caught a glimpse of Matt's neck while he continued to glance up at the moon. A large indent wrapped all around the middle of his neck...almost like a furrow mark.

"Jesus," Garrett said.

Matt looked down. "What?"

"What the hell happened to your neck?"

Matt quickly lost his smile too. He had been hoping that Garrett wouldn't notice the mark, but now that he had, Matt knew he was going to have to somehow talk his way out of it, so he quickly used his sharp mind and came up with a joke on the spot.

"Pressure."

Garrett got confused. "Pressure from what?"

Matt then looked into his eyes.

"Life...come on, let's get some pizza. I'm hungry now too," he said, changing the subject quickly.

Matt started to walk away while Garrett stood motionless, trying to piece together everything that was going on. While he had a few pieces of the puzzle together, he was still unable to make out the entire picture. And in that moment, told himself that they weren't leaving that beach until Matt started answering questions.

IX: Memories with Dinner

G arrett kept his eyes on Matt as Matt walked over to the sea wall he was sitting on. Matt lifted up the pizza box and two cans of soda for Garrett to grab and then got ready to jump up onto the wall.

"I've never heard of this place," Garrett said looking at the pizza box with skepticism.

Matt failed to get up onto the sea wall on his first try. Garrett looked down at him and smiled.

"Need help?"

"No, I'm good; how could you not have heard of Tripoli Pizza?" Matt asked as he finally made it up on the third try and sat down next to Garrett.

"Cause I eat normal food that tastes good."

Matt shook his head in disgust before opening the pizza box, revealing a beautiful cheese pizza and a smell that was nothing short of heavenly.

"Just try it before you dis it...you want an end piece or middle piece?"

"Surprise me."

Matt chuckled and started to pull apart an end piece, despite the end being his preferred choice.

"How'd you hear about this place?"

"Use to ride the motorcycle with my grandpa and come down here a lot during the summers off. It's been a while, that's for sure."

Garrett looked at Matt.

"Now, by riding with your grandfather, you mean..."

"Yes, I use to ride bitch on the back of his bike, asshole, so yeah, go ahead and judge me."

Garrett broke out into laughter. "You know that doesn't surprise me at all. I can totally see that."

"Just eat your pizza and shut up," Matt ordered as he handed Garrett the large slice.

Garrett took the piece from Matt and then lifted it up to his face, examining the way it looked.

"It doesn't look like any pizza I've ever had before."

Matt ripped a piece of pizza for himself and then lifted it

up to his mouth.

"Just try it already, you big baby."

Garrett shook his head, lifted up the slice and took a large bite right out of the middle. Instantly a taste that he had never tasted before filled his mouth (along with heat from the fresh pizza) and he couldn't help but smile knowing he would have to admit Matt was right about it.

"Holy shit...this is good pizza!" Garrett said before taking another huge bite into the slice.

"I told you!" Matt opened his can of Diet Soda and took a sip.

Garrett finished his mouthful of pizza. Before taking another bite he turned and looked at Matt. It was clear to him that their friendship had changed over the years and he didn't realize just how much until that moment. He brushed off his hands before looking up at the brilliant moon, the light shining down on them and lighting up the entire ocean before them as they ate.

"It's beautiful," Garrett confessed.

Matt crammed another large piece into his mouth and nodded. "Yes it is. Like something out of a post card."

Garrett smiled, looking down at the beach sand just below them.

"I gotta say. I doubted you for a while there."

Matt swallowed his pizza and looked at him, cracking open his can of soda. "What do you mean doubted?"

"I wasn't sure if this was going to be good or not."

Matt suddenly coughed after his soda went down the wrong pipe.

"The hell does that mean? When have I ever steered you wrong?" Matt began before clearing his throat.

"Well..." Garrett began before Matt interrupted him.

"About food! When have I steered you wrong about food?"

Garrett chuckled and then thought back, trying to decide on which food Matt had him try that he absolutely hated the most.

"Those nasty ass chips you made me try, for one."

"What nasty ass chips?"

"Those pickle and guacamole flavored chips you had when I came over."

Matt thought about it for a moment.

"Oh yeah. Okay I'll give that to you, those things tasted like shit. But that was just one thing, big deal," he said, taking another bite.

"Oh no, there's much more there, bud."

"Okay, name them then, if there's so many."

"The buffalo chicken wings, the cheese pie filled with onions, grilled mushrooms, strawberry cheesecake cookies and beef stew with enough salt to give someone a heart attack."

Matt thought about each thing he named off, and realized Garrett was right. Of course Matt wasn't going to admit that, though.

"There was nothing wrong with the cheesecake cookies!"

"They didn't even taste like cheesecake! They tasted like ass with a slice of American cheese on the side."

Matt instantly blew soda out of his mouth and started laughing. Garrett started laughing harder too, while his mind thought deeper into that night. And being so deep in memories, his mind didn't just stop at that night. It started to go back, way back to the beginning of high school when they met.

"Hey, you know what I was thinking?" Garrett asked as a

few more chuckles rolled out of him.

"What?" Matt asked as he handed Garrett one of the last pieces left.

"Our friendship started with a piece of gum."

Matt swallowed the large piece of pizza in his mouth, wiped the piece of cheese off of his lip and then looked at him.

"Magical right? What, you didn't know that?"

Garrett shrugged his shoulders.

"I mean I did, but I don't know, I guess I never really thought about it. Not recently anyway."

"Oh gee, thanks a lot pal."

"No, that's not what I meant. I meant like the small things like that. Guess I focused more on the bigger parts of our friendship rather than the little things."

"They always say it's the little things that count in life. You can't have a CEO if there's no paper pushers."

Garrett rolled his eyes with a slight smile.

"Come on. Why on Earth would I want to think about a piece of gum when I can think about tying your shoe laces together while you were sleeping in history class? Or when you slipped and fell into a puddle when we walked to my house after midterms?"

"That shoelace thing was a dick move, you ass!" Matt said with a chuckle.

Garrett started to laugh. "It was funny."

"I was on the third floor! I had to hop down three flights of stairs for my next class! Not to mention I had to cut the laces down to nothing in order to get the damn knot out of them."

Garrett laughed harder. "When was that anyway? Was that sophomore year?"

Matt hesitated before he answered, double checking and going through all the memories he collected over the years with Garrett, just to make sure the answer he had were right.

"No, it was junior year. We were in Mr. Van Uden's class then."

"Oh yeah, that's right. God was that funny."

"Yeah it was. Kinda scary that's coming up on ten years ago..."

Garrett lifted his eyebrows in amazement; beyond shocked that so much time had passed by without him even noticing.

"Wow, I didn't realize it had been that long. Damn."

"Yeah, time flies when you take your eyes off the clock," Matt said with a mouthful.

Garrett nodded in agreement.

"Yeah. Yeah, it does."

Matt took another sip of soda and smiled, chuckling under his breath.

"What?" Garrett asked when he saw the look on Matt's face.

"Oh, nothing; I was just thinking back to junior year...I think it was my favorite year out of all of them."

"Why's that?"

"Well, freshman year, I was fatter then Christ and had no friends. Sophomore year sucked until my schedule got changed and that was more than halfway through the school year and senior year I was addicted to drugs and got suspended the first day for drinking."

"I actually meant what about junior year made it so special, but that answer works too," Garrett said with a smirk.

"Oh!" Matt said with a laugh. "Now I get it. What made junior year so special to me?"

"Yeah."

The question echoed within Matt. He had known the answer for years, and after waiting so long for the right time, Matt knew in that moment the time was right. And when he lowered his head down from the moon and looked into Garrett's brown eyes, it was clear the funny side of Matt was pushed to the side and the real Matt emerged.

"You."

When the word sank in Garrett, like always, chose not to say anything. But in that moment he didn't have to. The answer was in his eyes as he smiled warmly at Matt. Matt returned the look as his heart began to beat heavily. After getting lost in the moment and in each other's eyes, Matt slowly started to lean in toward Garrett. Instead of resisting, like he would normally do, Garrett smiled, picked up the last piece of pizza, and put it in Matt's face.

"Eat your last piece of pizza, bud. Lord knows you stood in line long enough for the damn thing."

When Garrett mentioned the wait, Matt quickly put his hand in his left pocket. "Crap, I totally forgot!"

Garrett watched Matt dig into his pocket. "Forgot what?"

"Well, the wait was like twenty minutes, so I briefly popped into that creepy looking shop next door and got you something."

Garrett looked up at the shop, only to see that it really was a rundown junk store. He wondered what in the hell Matt could've picked up and bought there.

"What?" He asked nervously.

After digging in his pocket a little more, Matt grabbed a hold of the little container and pulled it out of his pocket. He looked at the clear top to make sure what was inside wasn't broken and, once he saw it was good, he then handed it to Garrett with a smile, hoping Garrett would like it.

Garrett took hold of the box and slowly lifted up the top, revealing a beautiful red glass clam shell. Garrett's eyes widened, taken aback by just how stunning it looked. He carefully grabbed a hold of the glass shell and lifted it up.

"I saw it by the window and...I don't know, I thought maybe you would like it."

"I do...it's pretty cool looking actually. I have a question though."

"It was three thousand dollars plus tax," Matt quickly said as he ate the last of the pizza.

"No, not that, you liar...I was going to ask what's inside the shell?"

Matt burped and then leaned in as Garrett held it up and passed it over to him. Matt looked carefully at it, but it didn't take him long to figure out what it was. "That's a pearl."

Garrett looked at it again and noticed it was a different color. At first he thought it was just the moonlight making it look different, but he decided to cover it with his hands and look through the little opening he made near his wrist. Then he saw why it looked like a different color.

"It glows in the dark!"

"Oh, nice! I actually didn't know it did that."

Garrett looked at it one more time and then placed it back in the box and carefully put it in his pocket.

"Thanks, buddy."

"Anytime."

Garrett kept his eyes on Matt as Matt looked all around, realizing that they seemed to be the only ones around on the beach.

"I believe you."

Matt turned and met Garrett's eyes with his own. "Believe

me about what?"

"The whole anytime thing.... you actually really mean it," Garrett began as he brought his attention out to the ocean. "Thinking about it now...you've always been there...you've always helped me. Whether it was helping me move or lending me money for rent..."

Matt nodded.

"It's you that's always been there. It's you that's never let me down...and it's been like that for years. Now I feel stupid that I've just never said that to you face to face before," Garrett finished.

"You never had to tell me...I knew...I can't explain it or even describe it really but I knew; I've known for a long time."

Garrett pulled his eyes away from Matt and lowered them as he felt tears building up. He had never cried in front of Matt in all the years they had known each other, and refused to start anytime soon.

Matt couldn't see Garrett's face or even his eyes but he didn't have to; he knew where Garrett, and his heart, was. It brought a smile to his face, but his heart hurt thinking about just how much time had been lost before Garrett had reached this point. But he tried not to dwell on that, he just tried to focus on where they were in that moment.

"Come on. Let's take a walk down by the water," Matt said as he put his arm around Garrett and then patted his shoulder.

Garrett looked up and smiled. "Alright, sounds good to me."

They stopped when a loud noise shot out through the air and lifted up into the sky. The two of them both looked to the sky when suddenly a large red firework exploded above, creating a smile on both of their faces as more and more started to enter the sky. Colors from red and green, to purple and gold lit up the entire beach in a way that neither one of them had ever seen before.

"And I thought my birthday party fireworks were cool!" Matt shouted over the noise.

Their eyes met for a brief moment before Matt suddenly looked up at the sky as another one went off, revealing the large indent around the lower part of his neck.

"Whoa, shit!" Matt said as he pointed up into the sky.

Matt's pointing quickly took Garrett's attention, forcing

him to look up and see not just one large firework go off, but two. Garrett glanced back at Matt's neck from the corner of his eye while Matt smiled and kept his head up until the fireworks finished and echoes vanished. He then elbowed Garrett in the stomach, clearly with excitement.

"Come on," he said and hopped off the sea wall and into the soft, light brown sand.

Garrett took a moment, thinking about the mark on Matt's neck. Then he thought about how Matt had consistently changed the subject when it came to any personal questions tonight. He remembered the conversation they'd had in the donut shop parking lot, when Matt asked about how they would spend their 'final nine'.

But the real clue for Garrett was Matt's neck. At first he hadn't even notice the mark, but when he first saw it, it brought up red flags. But it was seeing it up close that gave what was happening away. Garrett then shook his head in awe as a tear slid down his face, realizing that the sight of his scar had just revealed a number of things...including the way Matt had chosen to end his own life.

X: Answers

Matt was more than halfway down to the water before he turned and realized Garrett hadn't even gotten off the sea wall. He started to wonder and worry if something was wrong. The moonlight was bright but from the distance he was at, it was difficult for him to make out Garrett's face.

"You coming?!" Matt shouted up to him.

Matt's voice took Garrett out of his train of thought. He looked up at Matt and then jumped down onto the sand and walked towards Matt. He had every intention of demanding answers about everything. Garrett knew the time had come and all he could hope for was that Matt felt the same way, though he doubted it.

"Started to wonder why you were still hanging out up there," Matt began before he turned and looked down toward the beach. "Which way do you wanna head? If we head towards the bottom of the pier, I can show you where I pissed on a dead seagull back when I was in middle school."

Garrett shook his head in disappointment, and when Matt turned back around and saw Garrett's head and facial expression, it took him off guard.

"What, you wanna go the other way?" Matt asked sincerely.

Garrett exhaled and then looked back out towards the water.

"You know, this whole night, I've been trying to figure out what exactly has been going on here. At first I tried to figure out how you're here and showed up in my bedroom, when everyone said you were dead. Then I tried to start figuring out why you said that after tonight we can't see each other for a while. And no matter how hard I tried, I just couldn't figure it out. As the night's gone on and we've talked, laughed like we use to, it took my attention off figuring it all out. Hell I even stopped asking questions...like you said I should...but, then I saw your neck...and I figured it out," Garrett said with annoyance in his voice.

Matt chuckled and looked away as Garrett turned and looked at him.

"What the hell is so funny?" Garrett asked forcefully before

Matt turned back to him.

"You're saying that you've figured it out? You really think you've figured out everything? Well, let me tell you something: you don't know shit pal. This is a conversation that you're not ready or prepared for, so drop it before you ruin a good night." He turned and started walked towards the pier.

For the briefest of seconds, Garrett actually thought about taking Matt's advice again. He knew pressing on would pretty much ruin everything, and take away the fun of the night, but Garrett had to know, there was no two ways about it. He watched Matt, who was just about at the pier, and ran over to him as fast as he could. Then once he caught up to him, he roughly grabbed his arm and spun him around.

"What the fuck?" Matt shouted.

"Tell me why you're alive when everyone said you were dead," Garrett ordered.

"Oh Jesus Christ, give me a break..." Matt said, rolling his eyes.

"Don't give me that crap! You always do this! You drop hints about shit and then never have the balls to back any of them up! Now for once, you're gonna man up and answer me.

How in the hell are you alive?"

"Oh my God," Matt said in aggravation.

"How did you get your car back if your grandfather locked it up in his garage?"

"Really? You're going to do this now?"

"Why is this going to be the last time we see each other? Why do you keep dropping hints about something but not actually saying anything? And why the fuck does it look like a rope mark is all around your goddamn neck like everyone said there was?"

Matt grabbed Garrett and then pushed him away as hard as he could, angry that Garrett chose not to heed his warning.

"Why do you think?!" Matt shouted. "You really want the truth? Well here it is: this whole night isn't real! It's a dream you're having! I'm not really here, you're not really there. It's all one big goddamn dream going on inside your head. And as far as the mark on my neck, it *is* from a rope. A belt, actually. And why is that? It's because I really am dead. I did kill myself! Hung myself on an exercise machine at my work! It took three hours for someone to find me and that's why the mark is so deep! I tried cutting my wrist too, but when that didn't work, I went for the next best thing. I wrapped that belt around my neck and dropped myself! Hell I didn't even flinch or hesitate, in case you wanted to know. So, there it is...you happy now? You satisfied?"

The words echoed in the air, each one sinking into Garrett's mind as his chest began to feel heavy. It really was the answer he thought it would be, and it became another moment in his life where he wished he was wrong. But instead of focusing on the emotional side of the situation, he fixated on his anger and swung his fist into Matt's face, taking Matt off guard and dropping him down to his knees.

"Ow!" Matt said as he held his face and slowly stood back up. "You dick!"

"Really? Really? You kill yourself, leave me hanging and yet somehow I'm the dick," Garrett shouted said as Matt stood back up.

Matt shook his head and threw his hands up in the air.

"Oh give me a break! I waited for you to pull your head out of your ass for years and admit to yourself that you're gay, and I left you hanging? Please, you've left me hanging for years."

Garrett quickly shook his head, picking up on Matt's metaphor. "No, no. Don't you dare put you killing yourself on me! Don't put that on me!"

"No, I'm not talking about that, you idiot! I did that for my own reasons! I'm talking about you never saying anything or even acknowledging the fact about us, but yet somehow we could fuck every week and pretend like nothing ever happened! Eight goddamn years you've kept our relationship secret in the shadows from everyone and you were perfectly fine with that!"

"Now, wait a second..." Garrett began but quickly got cut off.

"No! I've done enough waiting. I put all these years on hold for you! I didn't get into any other relationships; I didn't go to college in Florida like I wanted to and I didn't become what I wanted to become. And all because I bogged myself down because for some reason I thought you would come around, stop denying everything and see what was right in front of you. I mean, do you know how hard it was to be around you and all your girlfriends and pretend like nothing was happening? Or having to try and pretend that knowing you were screwing them didn't affect me?" Matt asked, shouting at Garrett as loud as he could.

The more Matt went on about the past few years and everything he felt, the more Garrett started to realize how much he didn't notice. He began to wonder and even think that Matt's death was indeed, his fault. Or at least was a main factor. The thought of that shook him to the core, making his eyes fill up.

"I should've ended all this a long time ago like I said I would, but I just couldn't. Every time I would pull away, you would suddenly push closer and give me false hope...and all for nothing! Absolutely nothing!" Matt said as he shook his head in disgust before giving a final blow to a broken Garrett. "So I answered my question, now it's time for you to answer yours: why didn't you say anything? Why didn't you do anything if you really liked what we had?"

Matt turned back to Garrett and fixed his eyes on him. He assumed that Garrett wouldn't answer, just like any other time...and he didn't. Silence and the sound of the waves coming onto shore was the only thing to be heard. Once enough time passed, Matt threw his hands up in the air, turned and started to walk away.

Garrett heard Matt's footsteps walking away. He looked up, his eyes filling with heartache and tears. Deep in his heart, he knew the conversation about them was eventually going to pop up, even despite pushing it to the back burner and even forgetting about it for years. But he knew he couldn't remain silent anymore; he had to be honest with himself for the first time in his life.

"I was scared," he shouted, loud enough for Matt to hear.

Matt stopped walking, turned around and looked at him as Garrett's answered echoed in his mind.

"What?" He asked before making his way back over to Garrett.

Garrett took in a deep breath and repeated. "I was scared."

"Scared about what?"

"About being labeled! That people would judge me, look at me differently...I don't know. I was just buying time I guess. Trying to find out what I really wanted...and how to accept what it was that I wanted...okay? I wasn't trying to drag you along or anything like that. I was just buying time, alright? I don't know what you want me to say!" Garrett shouted as he shrugged his shoulders.

"Life isn't about buying time...it's about living with the time you've got."

And those would be the words that sent tears down Garrett's cheeks, unable to hide them from Matt any longer. He looked down and wiped them away, but Matt had already seen them. At first Matt tried to stand his ground and stay tough, but when he saw the pain and hurt in Garrett, he crumbled too, crying as he kept his eyes on Garrett. Matt slowly walked up to Garrett and opened his arms...and for the first time in their entire relationship, Garrett showed his true colors and leaned into Matt, wiping the tears off his cheek as he started to feel a warm, almost comfortable feeling inside. It was the first time Garrett had ever felt such a feeling with anyone. He couldn't explain the feeling, but somehow, someway, the moment felt perfect...like he was in a preview of what Heaven was supposed to be like.

Garrett finally decided that he wanted more, always had but could never find the way to say it. But in Matt's arms he was finally able to not only find his courage, but also his voice. Before Matt even knew what was even happening, Garrett lifted up his head and leaned into Matt, their warm lips meeting softly. Matt stopped questioning it when he realized exactly what Garrett was doing and returned the kiss, sliding his hands up Garrett's chest and up to his cheeks as Garrett rubbed the smooth hair on the back of Matt's head.

Despite wanting it for close to a decade, Matt was nervous about completely being with Garrett. He was afraid that he was going to do something wrong and screw something up. But the feeling was nowhere near as bad as what he thought it was going to be, the same with Garrett. It felt right, it felt strong, and most of all it felt like it should've happened a long time ago. But late was better than never at all.

With their lips locked together, both stood up and began walking under the pier in the moonlight. The moonlight wasn't strong enough to light up every area under the pier, but the cracks in the wood above were able to let patches of moonlight onto the sand throughout, providing just the right amount of light to guide them to the middle of the pier.

After another passionate kiss, Garrett lifted up his arms for Matt to pull his shirt off while Matt began to undo his belt. They kissed passionately again as Garrett undid Matt's zipper and pulled down his shorts, revealing what appeared to be Christmas boxers.

"Christmas underwear?" Garrett asked as looked down with a smile.

"Really? You pull down my pants and the first thing you do is question my underwear?" Matt shot back.

Garrett chuckled, forcing Matt to also chuckle as he kissed Garrett on the forehead before they locked lips again and fell onto the sand. The sand was warm and soothing as they rolled around, before Matt lifted himself up and sat up on Garrett's stomach. He then took off his shirt. Garrett looked up and smiled, the moonlight shining down upon his face. Matt leaned down and they kissed slowly, passionately, and in that moment it was clear that each of them were happier than they ever had been before.

It wasn't sex or hormones. It was friendship, happiness and most of all: love. Time doesn't stop for anything, but it does slow down every once in a while, the moment just has to be right...and Garrett and Matt had found their moment as they made love in the sand and under peaceful moonlight.

XI: Sunrise

The sound of a large wave crashing onto shore was what woke Garrett. Wiping the sleep from his eyes, he slowly lifted his head off his shirt and looked around. The beach was still empty, with nothing but birds roaming around for a meal. Garrett shook the sand out of his hair before putting his shirt back on, followed by his white socks. Once he was dressed, he suddenly realized he was alone; Matt was nowhere in sight.

Shaking the sand off him as he stood up, Garrett looked all around under the pier, making sure he wasn't missing Matt if he was under there. He walked out from under the pier and onto the beach, realizing Matt was nowhere to be found. Another large wave crashed onto shore and snatched his attention. But once the wave subsided, it was the distant horizon that he focused on.

It took a moment to get past the fact that the light blue and touch of yellow was breathtaking, but fear slowly started to build in his chest as he moved his eyes away from the view. The horizon indicated that the night was coming to an end and he wasn't sure what to make of it... or what it even really meant. He took in a deep breath of fresh ocean air and looked up at the beach wall and saw someone sitting on it. The beach wall was a good distance away but he was pretty sure it was Matt up there.

He walked over, feeling a bit tired but also energized for some unknown reason. But the tiredness blew over as he approached Matt, who was looking out toward the ocean, taking in the bright and brilliant glow of the sun approaching the horizon. He didn't take his eyes off the view, even as Garrett jumped up onto the wall.

Garrett was a little taken aback, it was rare to see Matt in such a calm, energized state in the morning. Normally, when Garrett would sleep over Matt's house, Matt would blast him out of bed at an unbearable hour. Garrett sat down next to him and softly tapped him on the shoulder. Matt broke away from the view, turned and met his eyes with a large smile before Garrett handed him the glass clam shell.

"Hey," he said.

"Hey," Garrett said as he kissed the top of Matt's head and nestled closer to him. "Amazing view, huh?"

"Oh yeah, I always wanted to watch the sun come up over the beach. There's just something about being the first one to see the sun come up that amazes me," Matt said, looking back to the horizon.

"Never looked at it like that before. Anyway, you let me fall asleep?" Garrett asked as he stretched.

"Yeah. You kinda fell asleep after and I didn't want to bother you, so I figured I'd let you be."

Garrett nodded and looked down at him. "You get any sleep?"

"No. I watched you for a while and when it got lighter out, I came up here. Besides, last time I fell asleep here, I woke up with nothing but sand all in my crack."

Garrett laughed, shaking his head. He looked out to the horizon, clearly able to see the sun slowly approaching in the distance. But the view wasn't what kept his mind occupied, it was the fact that nothing felt any different. Despite being with Matt every now and then for years, Garrett told himself that if they were anything more, then it all would change, the friendship, the laughs and the feelings he got when Matt was around. But to his amazement, that didn't turn out to be the case.

"Been up here long?"

Matt nodded.

"No, maybe a half hour. It was a bitch to get up here again, but yeah probably a half hour."

Garrett lowered his head, looking down at the sand and then at Matt's bare feet. "This is probably the first time I've ever seen you with your shoes off," Garrett confessed.

"Yeah well don't get used to it, they got wet last night so I'm waiting for them to dry. Once they are, they're going right back on."

Garrett shook his head, chuckling underneath his breath.

"You're weird," he said as he patted Matt on the back.

"That's why you love me," Matt shot right back.

Garrett laughed and looked around the quiet beach as Matt began to slowly lose his smile and look down.

"Hey..." he began, grabbing Garrett's attention. "About what I said last night...I just wanted to say that I'm..."

"No, you don't have to apologize. I'm the one who's sorry,"

Garrett quickly responded back.

"You have nothing to be sorry for. And when I implied what happened was your fault about...me... I'm sorry. I should never have said that. It was a shit move to do."

Garrett nodded, trying his best to be supportive as Matt's suicide came back up. Matt briefly looked at Garrett and then back out to the water, knowing what he was about to say would answer any remaining questions Garrett had.

"Looking back, I still can't believe I did it. I mean I thought about it for years and really started looking into it about a year or so before, but honestly...I still can't believe I did it. I know a lot of people think it was planned and in a way I guess you could say it was, but it wasn't. It was honestly one of those heat of the moment things. Guess that's what bipolar does to you. You see bipolar is black and white. You gotta figure, if black is every color and white is no color...then that's exactly what bipolar is, it either feels like you have everything or it feels like you have nothing. And that morning, I felt I had nothing..."

Matt's words hit Garrett hard, his eyes watering, forcing him to look up into the early morning sky. He thought about telling Matt to stop where he was at, but he couldn't. He needed to hear the rest of the story...and the answers he needed.

"Probably about a month before, I was in one of those moods and I really thought about it. I wasn't planning on doing anything at that point, but I gave some thought about where I would do it because I tried it at home and it didn't work; the damn belt fell off the doorknob," Matt told Garrett. "So after some serious thinking, I decided the best place would be at my work, in the exercise room. No one normally went in there in the mornings, and it wouldn't be at home, which I think is the main reason why I chose to do it there. I know my Mom and I always had problems but to force her to see that would be awful and I knew I couldn't hurt her like that."

Garrett sniffled softly as tears fell off his cheeks and onto the soft sand just below them.

"I was able to get into work that morning about an hour early, before anyone else showed up. I got into the exercise room, closed the door, closed all the shades and just stood in the darkness. And then everything hit me...it's amazing what darkness can reveal. All the fights with my Mom, the fight I was in with my grandparents. But the thing that I really thought about was how everyone always would say to me that I'm a catch, I'm an awesome person, I'm attractive and I have a great personality...and yet I was alone and lost with so many emotions wearing me down inside. I'd been fighting with the doctors to change my meds for weeks but it started to feel like a lost cause. That's when I realized how alone I really was. No one was there...and in that moment, neither was I. And that's what did it...that's what pulled me into the shadows..."

Tears slowly ran down Matt's face as he did his best to keep his voice from cracking, but it was getting tough. In the corner of his eye he could see that what he was saying was hitting Garrett hard too. Inside, Matt knew it would be hard for Garrett to hear what happened, but he also knew that he needed to hear it.

It took Garrett some time to clear his throat and get the tears to slow before he was able to look up Matt. But no matter how hard he tried to get his tears under control, they kept coming when he thought about Matt in that exercise room, looping the belt around the handle on the exercise machine, putting it around his neck and then dropping...it was a hard image for him to grasp.

"I'm sorry Matt..." Garrett began as he put his arm around his best friend. "I'm so sorry I wasn't there."

Matt finally took his eyes off the ocean and lowered them to Garrett, as Garrett lowered his head into his hand.

"I've struggled with things inside for close to seven years, even remember when they started. Every day I searched for something that would keep me going. Sometimes it was hard to find something new in my life. I mean after all, I was trying to go out and meet new people, get a new job, get a new car...so you would think that I'd be happy! But I never could, nothing seemed to stick for me. Yeah sure, all those times gave me temporary moments of something but it was never real. It wasn't something I could look back on and say to myself: 'yeah, that's when it all changed.' Who knows, maybe you only get one of those types of feelings in life and maybe I was stupid to try and duplicate it...to try and capture lighting in a bottle twice. But in all those years and all those thoughts, I did have one thing that I could fall back on when the rest of the world let me down. And that was you. Even today, it's still hard to explain, but being around you takes away those feelings of disappointment in my life. You provide me with laughs, smiles...love. I know we have our share of arguments and I piss you off, but I know they never mean anything and that's what I love about what we have. The first time we did stuff to each other, it didn't feel awkward afterward. Even the next time we saw each other at school, everything felt the same. No tension, no weirdness...still just friends. And that was the moment for me, that was when it all changed for me. You were that moment for me; that lightning in a bottle. And that's what I focused on throughout these past couple of years. It kept me going. You kept me going and ultimately kept me fighting and holding on for as long as I did," Matt explained as Garrett looked up at him, taking it all in. "So don't be sorry. Don't ever be sorry. You gave me light when I was lost in the shadows."

Matt then took his eyes off the ocean and looked at his both heartbroken but honored partner; smiling at him before wiping the last tears off Garrett's face with his thumb. Garrett closed his eyes as Matt wiped the pain away. When he felt

Matt's thumb move off his face, Garrett opened his eyes and locked eyes with Matt. They leaned in and shared a long, powerful and romantic kiss together...just as the top half of the sun emerged on the horizon and caste a warm, bright glow over the two.

Once they pulled away from each other, they looked back into each other's eyes and smiled, almost chuckling to one another as Garrett lowered his head, softly placing it on Matt's left shoulder and took hold of his hand.

Garrett also smiled, looking down at Matt's hand. He noticed a mark on Matt's wrist just below his hand. Curious, he softly turned over Matt's hand, getting Matt's attention and causing him to look down.

Once Garrett saw what it was, he looked into Matt's blue eyes. Matt wasn't really sure how to respond at first, he had a difficulty reading the expression on Garrett's face. It was clear he looked bothered, but Matt hoped Garrett wouldn't make anything out of it.

There were five very long and deep looking scars across his wrist, clearly symbolizing what Matt had tried to do before choosing a different method. It was difficult to see, but Garrett felt like there was nothing more to say about it. So instead of causing another fight and ruining the moment they were in, he chose to simply lift Matt's wrist up to his face and softly kiss the scars.

The gesture brought a tear to Matt's eye before lowering his head down and resting his chin on the top of Garrett's head. When Garrett finally lifted up his head and looked up at a smiling Matt, they went in for another deep kiss.

"Can I ask you something?" Garrett asked after pulling away and resting his head back on his shoulder.

"Yes, I know I'm a good kisser," Matt quickly shot out. "Ask me whatever you want."

Scared at first to even ask, Garrett reminded himself that if anyone were to tell him the truth and be honest, it would be Matt. And knowing that gave him the courage to ask the question he's always thought about. "Is there a Heaven?"

"Yes," Matt quickly responded.

Garrett closed his eyes in relief—happy that his biggest fear in life was answered.

Despite the fact that Matt answered so quickly, he didn't even realize that he had just provided Garrett with something that would shape how he would live the rest of this life.

"...What's it like?"

Matt smirked as he began to think about his. "Imagine the happiest moment of your life. The moment where everything aligned perfectly. Then think about that feeling you got during that moment and how you wished the moment would've lasted forever..." Matt began before he turned to Garrett. "That moment and feeling is what Heaven is. A lot of people think it's a long stairway to the top of the sky with gates and a large kingdom, but it's not. We create our Heaven while we're alive...and we live it when we die."

Garrett smiled as he thought about the idea of it all. It was a lot to take in, but he was fine. He felt like he had just won the Powerball. But there was one other thing that Garrett was curious about. He knew it was probably not his business but he decided to ask anyway because he wanted to get all the answers.

"What did you choose?"

"June 22nd 2013. It was the day we..."

"Had your birthday party and lit off all those fireworks. Damn near blew us and the house up because of how big those suckers were. We spent the whole day together and the whole night," Garrett finished.

Matt turned his head, surprised by not only Garrett's answer but also the fact that he remembered details. "You remember that?"

"Of course, why wouldn't I?"

Matt shrugged his shoulders and answered without trying to sound rude. "I guess I just never thought you were paying such close attention."

"You'd be surprised what I paid attention to over the years."

They exchanged one last kiss before Garrett wrapped his arm around Matt's shoulders and both looked out at the view as pinks, blues, oranges and light blues filled the sky in a way neither of them had ever seen before. Everything was perfect for some time, until Matt slowly began to pull away from the view and started to think about what this actually meant. He had been in the same position with Garrett when he was alive—enjoying the moment but knew what had to come next. But unlike the last times, Matt took a deep breath and figured he'd give Garrett a little more time to enjoy himself before he had to end it. And as he pulled his mind and attention away from the future, Matt held onto to Garrett tighter and in those brief seconds, even he forgot about what was coming next for the two of them.

XII: Heading Back

"Why would I want to get a coffee with two and two?" Matt asked as he pulled up to the drive thru of a coffee shop just before the turn to leave the beach. He was still mad over the large mark and dent on Garrett's door.

"So that way you can actually drive around and make it to places without having to worry your bowels are going to blow up on the way," Garrett quickly answered.

"Oh horseshit, I don't have that problem."

"Oh yeah?"

"Yeah!"

"You've never had that problem?"

"Well..."

"See! I told you. So trust me, just order two and two and forget about your normal coffee. This will be your normal coffee."

"I like my ten and ten!"

"There's not even coffee in there!"

"Exactly!"

Garrett shook his head in amazement as he looked at Matt's stubborn face. "Um why would you get coffee if you don't want to taste it?"

Matt rolled his eyes.

"I don't drink for the pleasure; I drink for the effect...same as a prostitute," he said before focusing on the drive thru menu board.

"What???" Garrett shouted out in confusion.

"Okay, bad analogy, but you get what I mean!"

"Yeah...I really don't, though."

Matt ended up taking Garrett's advice and trying the two and two coffee. Garrett even ordered one too, so that way Matt didn't feel like he was being suckered into it. And to Garrett's amazement Matt even ordered both of them a breakfast sandwich with a side of hash browns too (Matt usually did not allow food in the car). But since Matt had spilled his coffee, ruined the paint on his trunk, and now had a large indent and scrapes along the passenger side, it was clear that his pride and joy was no more.

They left the parking lot of the coffee shop and made their way onto the highway as Garrett took a large bite out of his sandwich and Matt took a sip of his boiling hot coffee. The further they drove away from the beach, the darker the sky got, something Garrett had never noticed before. Then again, he had never stayed overnight at a beach before.

"How's your sandwich?"

"Good," Garrett said through a mouthful. A large hunk of cheese fell out of the sandwich and landed on the seat. "How's your coffee?"

"Well, it tastes like coffee."

"Yeah and Skittles taste like Skittles."

"Great, now I'm in the mood for Skittles. Except for the green ones. Ever since they changed the flavor, it tastes like ass."

Garrett nodded as he lifted his head up from the hunk of cheese in between his legs.

"Seriously though, you like it?"

"I'm not telling you."

"Why?" Garrett asked as he planned out what he was going to do with the cheese on the seat.

"Because you're going to say I told you so," he answered back with a grin.

"Told you!" Garrett said as he patted Matt on the shoulder. "Would I steer you wrong?"

"You do, normally."

Garrett chuckled before looking up through the sunroof, taking in the dark blue sky as Matt headed back onto the highway. For the first time in his life, Garrett felt happy, happier than he'd ever been in his whole life. From the smile on Matt's face to a warm, relaxing feeling in his stomach, it was apparent to him that the meaning and goal of life was to be as happy as he was in that moment.

"Where to now? Breakfast? Sightseeing? I'm pretty much down for anything...as long as it's not another round of Go Karts. We're lucky both of us survived the first round."

Matt briefly smiled as he kept his eyes on the road.

"There something special you wanna do?" Garrett asked after pushing the piece of cheese off his seat and onto the floor.

Matt softly inhaled as all the things he wanted to do with Garrett circled around his head, some even placing a smile on his face for a second.

"Wish we had time," Matt said as he exhaled.

Instantly, Garrett was confused, questioning why Matt would say something like that when it was so early in the morning.

"What do you mean you wish we had more time? It's not even six in the morning. We've got the whole day!" Garrett said, admiring the colors of the morning sky from the sunroof.

Matt exhaled lightly after taking another sip of coffee. "We've gotta get you home."

"Why?"

"Because the sun is coming up."

"Yeah. So?"

"So, you need to be back at your house by the time it's up."

Garrett finally realized what Matt meant.

"Oh..."

The tone of Garrett's voice was much deeper, clearly filled with disappointment, and it caused Matt to take his eyes off the road and look at him. But instead of giving a big speech about life and time, he decided to fall back on what he's always done best: make Garrett laugh.

"I can't believe my goddamn car."

Garrett chuckled. "You're the one that wanted coffee."

"You're the one that distracted me at the mini golf place!"

"I was telling you to use your back up camera, but you didn't want to!"

"I didn't need it."

"Tell that to your trunk!"

"Yeah? Tell that to my door!"

Garrett chuckled, shaking his head before turning out towards the passenger window.

"You're stubborn," he quickly shot back at Matt.

"I am not."

"Oh yes to Christ you are. You're probably the stubbornest person I've ever met."

"That's a lie! You wanna know what I am? I'm..." Matt began before the back window finally gave way and shattered, sending glass flying out behind the car, all over the highway and pieces into the back seat.

Garrett snapped his head back to look at where the window used to be, while Matt glared at it through the rear view mirror.

"I'm without a back window, that's what I am," Matt said as he rolled his eyes and focused back onto the road while Garrett laughed.

Matt took another mouthful of his coffee and tried to relax, but it didn't work at first. It took Garrett reaching over and grabbing his hand to calm him down. Instantly Matt smiled, causing Garrett to do the exact same thing. Just by the looks on their faces, it was clear that they both had found that one person people always look for: a soulmate. But since Matt knew Garrett wasn't a touchy feely person, he chose to end the moment the same way Garrett would always end it when he tried making a move towards him.

"Oh, stop it. People will start talking about us," Matt joked in the grisliest voice he could.

Garrett shook his head. "Sometimes I wonder about you..."

"Oh my God, that's so sweet of you to say, I'm blushing almost as much as my penis is," he said with the same girly voice.

Garrett let go of his hand and picked up his coffee from the cup holder. "Oh shut it."

Matt burst into laughter. And his laugh was so infectious,

Garrett couldn't help but laugh with him as they made their way back home.

II

The car ride home seemed to go much faster than the ride to the beach. Maybe it was because they didn't stop for Go Karts on the way back. Maybe it was because Matt drove faster on the way back or maybe it was simply just the fact that they talked the whole way home, talking about everything from the days in high school to the darker ones where they stopped talking to each another for a while. When they pulled up to the driveway of Garrett's place, it was clear that despite it all, the reason they would always come back to one another was love.

"Boy my ass is sore. Never realized how uncomfortable these damn car seats are," Matt said as he groaned and stretched.

"I never did either. I also didn't realize how many times your ears pop if you don't have a back window," Garrett said as he got out of the car.

"My ears didn't pop, but my ass cheek fell asleep somewhere near Epping. And I'm not talking about a part of it; I'm talking the entire thing!" Matt shot back as he started to feel his behind.

"Maybe that was from last night..." Garrett said with a sarcastic smile.

Matt snapped his head. "I could tell you the same thing pal."

They laughed and closed the doors to the Dart before walking to the front of the car. Garrett kept on going but Matt stayed by his car, contemplating what he was going to do next as he watched Garrett make his way to the house. By the time Garrett noticed Matt wasn't behind him, he was already at the door of his house.

"You coming in?" He asked after unlocking the door and turning around.

"You want me to?" Matt shot back.

"Really? You have to ask that?"

Matt slightly smiled and then ran up to the door as Garrett held it open for him.

"Thanks, buddy. So thoughtful of you," Matt said in a softer girl voice.

Garrett chuckled. "Shut up."

Matt finished up the last of his snickering just as he reached the living room of Garrett's mom's house. As they looked around, both were surprised as to how dark it still was in the house despite the sky quickly changing over to light blue.

"Christ, it's just as dark in here now as it was when we left," Matt said.

"Tell me about it. I've been living here with her for almost a year and I still bang into things," Garrett said before a sudden bang lifted into the room.

"Ow! Goddamn it," Matt quietly said, rubbing his leg after banging it into a recliner.

Garrett laughed as they made their way into the kitchen. "There's a recliner there, bud."

"This part of the house always has the same smell to it; only this part though. The other part smells entirely different," Matt said.

Garrett thought about it for a minute while he walked over to his bedroom door and realized...Matt was right. Only the kitchen smelt nice.

"I actually never thought of that before. Now that you mention it though, you're right. That is really weird. Now I'm never going to forget that. Thanks bud."

"Anytime. That's what I'm here for...Ow!" Matt quickly said as his hip banged into the side of the kitchen table.

Garrett briefly turned. "Jesus Christ, what'd you hit this time?"

"My hip."

"How the hell did you do that?"

"Well for one; it's darker then Christ in here. I probably have a better chance of not hitting anything if I closed my eyes. And two, my ass-cheek is still asleep."

"Dear God, are we really gonna have a conversation about your ass cheek at six in the morning?"

"What's wrong with my ass-cheek at six in the morning?"

"I don't want to talk about your ass-cheek at six in the morning!"

"Well for your information, there's nothing wrong with my ass-cheek! Sure it might currently have a pimple on it the size of Rudolph's nose and more hair then the dudes on Duck

Dynasty, but it's still a nice looking ass cheek pal."

Garrett rolled his eyes as he opened his bedroom door and walked in.

"What am I going to do with you?"

"Oh you'd probably try selling me on the black market if you knew you could get away with it," Matt said walking in and looking around the messy room. "You'll have to give me the name of your housekeeper."

"It's a work in progress."

"Never would've guessed that...like at all."

"Funny," Garrett said as he walked over to his window shade and opened it, letting in the mild brightness of the morning, lighting up the room well enough to see.

He briefly looked out into the messy yard. Despite the fact that nothing at the house was perfect, he was okay with that. The yard held many memories for him, from showing his baby sister how to ride a bike to the first real date him and Matt had together. Taking his eyes off of the yard, he turned and stood over his bed before looking at Matt.

For a moment they stayed silent. Neither one really knew what to say despite knowing what the next conversation was going to be...but they both knew it had to be done.

"Well, this was an interesting night, kinda like I thought it was going to be," Matt said, breaking the ice and tension.

Garrett chuckled, crossing his arms around his chest.

"It really was, that's for sure."

Matt smiled when Garrett looked up into his eyes.

"Just like old times."

"Yeah, just like old times..." Garrett began as what was about to happen next started to really sink in.

Matt briefly pulled his eyes off Garrett and looked out the window, noticing how fast it was getting bright out. The end of the night had indeed come, causing his eyes to water as he took them off the window and looked back at the love of his life, only to realize his eyes weren't the only ones that were glossy.

Between friends and family, Garrett had lost a lot of people in his young life. Some were harder than others, but when he had found out about Matt, he had shattered as a pain so deep and crippling broke everything inside him. It was a pain like no other, and he hoped that he would never have to feel that great pain again...but looking into Matt's eyes and knowing the question he had to ask started bringing those feelings right back. But he knew he had to ask, despite already having an idea of what the answer was.

"I'm not going to remember any of this...am I?" Garrett asked, and his voice started to crack towards the end of the heavy question.

While he braced for the answer, Matt braced for Garrett's reaction. He knew this was the moment where he had to put away the funny side of him and reveal the caring and promising side of him.

"You're gonna get a feeling when you wake up, a feeling like you've never had before. It'll be hard to explain...but it'll give you something inside, reminding you that everything is gonna be okay. And it's that feeling that will get you through the next few months and ultimately be the reason why you'll be able to move on. But no, you won't remember this."

Tears began to run down his face as Garrett put his hand under his chin, trying to somehow grasp what Matt said. But he simply couldn't; the pain was just too damn hard to let anything in. He knew that and so did Matt, who was also having a hard time trying to keep himself together.

Tear drops landed on the floor as Matt slowly stepped toward Garrett, opened his arms and put them around Garrett's waist. Garrett returned the gesture—quickly wrapping his hands around Matt's shoulders, taking hold of his boy as the love in their hearts surrounded them one last time.

Matt knew it was going to have to come to this, and he knew the moment would be hard, but he never realized just how hard it would be. And it got even harder as Garrett kissed the side of his neck just before they both pulled back from one another and made eye contact.

Matt quickly wiped his eyes and cheeks, doing his best to try and stay strong for Garrett, but it was clear that nothing could help him...just like nothing could help Garrett either. The hard part had arrived.

They made eye contact again. Matt smiled at him and Garrett attempted to do the same, but he simply couldn't. The thought of losing Matt again was unbearable for him, just like the thought of leaving Garrett again was crippling for Matt. But in the end neither one could change what was happening, the time to change anything had come and gone. And as they looked at each other in what would be their final moments together, neither of them said it, but it was clear that they both deeply regretted the decisions they had made in their lives.

"Come on...let's get you into bed," Matt said.

Garrett wiped his eyes and took a deep breath—knowing what he had to do. He took his shirt off, followed by his shoes and then his shorts. For the first time in their friendship, Matt looked away not only to give Garrett privacy but also to get his sobs under control.

Garrett lifted up the blankets and got into the bed. Matt turned when he heard the covers lift up and then walked over as Garrett softly rested his head on the pillow, looking up at the ceiling as he sniffled. He looked back down when Matt sat next to him at the edge of the bed.

When he saw another tear running down Garrett's face, Matt lifted his hand up and softly wiped it away with his thumb, smiling down at Garrett while he did.

"No more tears...kinda like the Ozzy Osbourne song," Matt said with a little grin.

Garrett chuckled and took hold of Matt's hand and softly

rubbed his thumb across the front of his hand. It tickled Matt at first but he quickly got used to the feeling as Garrett kept doing it.

"Will I see you again?" Garrett asked with a broken voice.

"I think you already know the answer to that," Matt said as he lifted his eyes up off of his hand and looked to Garrett's. Matt leaned in and kissed him on the lips. Butterflies flew through them as the feeling of love echoed in and around their souls. The kiss was long, passionate and most of all: perfect, just like the rest of the night was. And it was the perfect way to close their little journey.

Matt slowly pulled away and lifted himself back up as he rubbed Garrett's soft light brown hair. "Time to go to sleep, bud."

Garrett shook his head just as Matt stood up and took a few steps towards the door. But before he got too far Garrett said his final words.

"I love you..."

The words echoed into Matt, stopping him in his tracks. He turned back around and looked down. Just by the look on Garrett's face, it was clear that Garrett wanted to say a lot more...but he didn't know how to phrase it.

"Just...don't forget that."

Matt nodded, knowing exactly what Garrett meant by the small yet meaningful sentence. It provided Matt with some closure and something inside for him to hold onto. And with that, Matt then said his final words.

"I'll be waiting for you...like I always have."

And with Matt's familiar words locked in his mind, Garrett softly closed his eyes and let sleep take over. And just like junior year of high school, Matt watched him, making sure he was asleep and was comfortable. And once it was clear that he was, Matt started for the door.

But before he reached the doorway, he suddenly began to feel something rubbing up against him through his pocket. Forgetting what was there, Matt slid his hand into his pocket and pulled the object out. It was the glass clam shell with the pearl inside he bought Garrett at the beach, the clear pearl glowing a soft yet bright green.

He turned around to hand it to Garrett, but when he saw that he was sleeping, he knew he couldn't...so he did the next best thing. He quietly walked back over and then softly placed it down on the small nightstand next to the bed. A smile grew on his face watching Garrett peacefully sleeping. The sight brought happiness into Matt's once lost heart, making him feel more alive than ever.

But before he could walk away, he took one last look at the love of his life, smiling at him the way couples always do after years and years of marriage. Despite the regret inside about his choices, Matt still smiled knowing that even though they'd be apart for a while, it wouldn't last forever. The only thing that would last forever would be how they felt about each other. Matt knew that...and he was so happy that after all the years as friends...Garrett was able to finally say it, and start living the way he'd always wanted. And with a final glance at his boy, Matt turned and walked out of the bedroom and outside, towards his car and the illuminating light at the end of the driveway.

Epilogue

It was a combination of the birds chirping and the sun shining into the bedroom that woke Garrett. With his eyes only half open, he reached over to his cell phone on the night stand and checked the time. It was only six thirty, but despite not having to be up for another half hour, Garrett chose to get up, stretching as he lifted himself up.

He started to notice a smell entering the room. It was a smell that Garrett instantly recognized and caused his stomach to growl as he wiped the sleep out of his eyes. The smell was bacon, one of the best smells to wake up to as Garrett would always say. Before he tried to get up so he could get ready for work, he yawned.

He couldn't place it or understand it, but for some reason he still felt tired; almost exhausted, even though he went to bed and fell asleep much earlier than he normally did. But as he thought about why, he kept getting these weird feelings, almost memories in his head. He couldn't place them or even explain them but they reminded him of Matt for some unknown reason. The more he thought about it, the more the strange feeling began emerging. It was a feeling like he had never gotten before and as more and more clips of these memories played in his mind, he started to figure out what the feeling was. For the first time in his young life, he started to not feel afraid if people found out about how he wanted to live his life.

The feeling made him a bit uncomfortable, but it also made him almost feel good, almost like things were somewhat back to normal despite the fact that Matt was gone and somehow, it would get better eventually. The feeling stuck with him all the way up until he got dressed just before a knock on the door grabbed his attention.

"Come in."

The door squeaked loudly before opening all the way as Katie stepped in.

"Hey you. How'd you sleep?" She asked with a hopeful look across her face.

Garrett nodded as he looked at her. "Not too bad. How'd

you sleep?"

Katie sighed. "I got in late. A lot of drama at the restaurant but by the time I got in, you were already fast asleep and I didn't want to wake you, so I slept on the couch in the living room."

Garrett smiled before turning around toward the dresser and sprayed two squirts of cologne onto his neck. As he finished up getting ready for work, he actually felt somewhat better, he was even getting his appetite back; something that he had lost days ago. But even though his spirt seemed a little higher than it had been recently, Katie didn't seem convinced that he was better.

"How you holding up?" She asked.

"Actually, feeling better today believe it or not. Maybe a good night's sleep is what I really needed."

Katie agreed as she walked over to him and kissed his cheek.

"Good. Glad to hear. You hungry?"

Garrett smiled. "Yeah, think I could eat a little this morning."

Katie quickly smiled.

"Good. Well why don't you finish up in here and come on out. Uncle Pete just got here about ten minutes ago, so if you want any bacon, I suggest you get to it before him," she chuckled.

Garrett grinned, knowing just how true that statement was.

"What's he doing here?" Garrett asked as Katie made her way out of the bedroom.

"Your Mom called him. She said she had a big announcement to share with everyone. She probably got that promotion at work, but she wants everyone to hear about it all at once..." Katie began as Garrett turned his head in curiosity. "I don't know; all she said is that sometimes it's best for people to find out things all at once, says it makes taking in the news a little easier. One way to look at it, right?"

Garrett softly nodded and looked back before he picked up his cell and put it in his pocket.

"Well finish up in here handsome, so we can get some food in you," she said with a smile before walking out of the room.

Garrett picked up his worn out wallet from the nightstand while what Katie said replayed in his head. The more he thought about it, the more he realized that his Mom was right. Having everyone find something out all at once wouldn't make the news easier to say, but at least it would get everything out in the open, clear the air, and not have to worry about who knew and who didn't know; something that Garrett feared for nearly a decade. But that morning there was no fear or any type of hesitation...or even desire to keep things a secret anymore.

"You ready to come out, babe?" Katie shouted from the kitchen as she made Garrett a plate of bacon and eggs.

He looked up and into a small mirror next to him, staring deeply into his own eyes, almost as if he was checking to make sure the courage on the inside was there on the outside. And as the warm light of the morning sunshine lit up his face, he quickly found his answer.

"Yeah, I'm ready," he said to himself before clearing his throat.

And once he took a final look at himself in the mirror and felt comfortable with what he was about to do, Garrett picked up his truck keys, placed them in his pocket and walked into the kitchen. And while he began explaining what was really in his heart, back in the bedroom on the nightstand, the red glass clam shell sat peacefully in the morning sunshine, with the clear pearl absorbing enough light to glow next to Garrett as he slept, for many nights to come, proving that the only thing stronger than the bond of friendship, is the power of love.

www.ingramcontent.com/pod-product-compliance
Lightning Source LLC
Chambersburg PA
CBHW050844180626
46814CB00007B/2609